I0748220

MONTANA
WYOMING
NORTH DAKOTA
MINNESOTA
IOWA
NEBRASKA
46°
45°
44°
43°
97°
98°
99°
100°
101°
102°
103°
104°
ROBERTS
Sisseton
MARSHALL
Britton
DAY
Webster
BROWN
Aberdeen
MCPHERSON
Leola
Mound City
CAMPBELL
McIntosh
CORSON
WALWORTH
Selby
EDMUNDS
Ipswich
SPINK
Redfield
Clark
CLARK
CODINGTON
Watertown
Milbank
GRANT
DEUEL
Clear Lake
HAMLIN
Hayti
BROOKINGS
Brookings
KINGSBURY
De Smet
BEADLE
Huron
MINER
Madison
LAKE
Howard
MOODY
Flandreau
MINNEHAHA
Sioux Falls
Parker
TURNER
MCCOOK
Salem
HANSON
Alexandria
DAVISON
Mitchell
SANBORN
Woonsocket
JERAULD
AURORA
Plankinton
HUTCHINSON
Olivet
BON HOMME
Tyndall
YANKTON
Yankton
CLAY
Vermillion
UNION
Elk Point
Canton
LINCOLN
Flandreau
FAULK
Faulkton
HAND
Miller
HYDE
Highmore
POTTER
Gettysburg
SULLY
Onida
HUGHES
Pierre
Fort Pierre
STANLEY
BUFFALO
Gannvalley
Wessington Springs
BRULE
Chamberlain
CHARLES MIX
Lake Andes
Armour
DOUGLAS
Burke
GREGORY
TRIPP
Winner
LYMAN
Kennebec
JONES
Murdo
MELLETTE
White River
TODD
BENNETT
Martin
SHANNON
JACKSON
Kadoka
HAAKON
Philip
ZIEBACH
Dupree
DEWEY
Timber Lake
PERKINS
Bison
HARDING
Buffalo
BUTTE
Belle Fourche
MEADE
LAWRENCE
Sturgis
Deadwood
PENNINGTON
Rapid City
CUSTER
Custer
FALL RIVER
Hot Springs
SOUTH DAKOTA
CITIES   BOUNDARIES
State capitals —— State
County seats —— County
0   15   30   45   60 mi
0 20 40 60 80 km
©1998, Encyclopaedia Britannica, Inc.

BECAUSE THEY LOVED HIM

BECAUSE THEY LOVED HIM

TRACI KAY DAVIS

First published in 2025 by Hambone Publishing
www.hambonepublishing.com.au

Editing by Mish Phillips and Lexi Wight
Interior design by David W. Edelstein

For information about this title, contact:
books@hambonepublishing.com.au
www.hambonepublishing.com.au

ISBN 978-1-922357-89-2 (paperback)
ISBN 978-1-922357-90-8 (ebook)

Preface

According to the South Dakota Governor's website, over 900 children are in foster care in South Dakota. Eighty-five children are waiting to be adopted. More than half of these children will experience at least seven different school changes during their time in the welfare system.

Statistics from the National Crimes Against Children's Investigative Association (NCACIA) reveal an alarming reality: Native American and Indigenous groups make up just 2% of the total U.S. population, yet they account for 15.2% of child abuse cases. This means Native and Indigenous children are seven times more likely to be subjected to physical abuse, sexual abuse, neglect, or a combination of these hardships.

My name is Traci Loecker. For seven years, I have served as a Court Appointed Special Advocate (CASA). Out of the five cases I have worked on, three involved Native American children. I have also provided emergency kinship placement for a ten-year-old child. The children I have worked with have ranged in age from six months to fifteen years old.

Over the years, my experiences as a CASA have profoundly shaped my perspective. I have learned so much, and through this book, I want to share some of the most impactful moments from my cases. I also wrote a love letter to my CASA kids.

I became a CASA in 2017. My first case involved a two-year-old girl and her six-month-old baby brother. Their mother was just 18 or 19 years old and had spent her entire life in a group home. As a CASA, my role was to be an impartial advocate for the children, providing the court with recommendations based on the children's best interests.

After months of meeting with the young mother, foster parents, social workers, and attorneys, I had to make a heartbreaking recommendation about where these children should be placed. It was through this case that I realized love sometimes means letting go—allowing children to have the life they deserve, even if their parents cannot provide it. I never doubted this young mother's love for her children. And she proved her love by making the hardest decision a parent can make: letting them go.

In 2019, I received a phone call from a friend I had lost touch with. She admitted she was addicted to meth and was in outpatient therapy. I advised her to seek inpatient care, but I also told her I would help however I could.

A few weeks later, she called again. This time, her request was urgent: "Will you take G for me?"

Without hesitation, I said yes.

She then handed the phone to a Department of Social Services (DSS) agent. Only later did I learn that this conversation had taken place at a police station—she had been arrested. The DSS agent explained that taking G would mean at least 30 to 45 days of care, possibly longer. I agreed without question.

Now, I had to tell my husband and children that our lives were about to change.

When I told my husband, Doug, he asked, "How old is she?"

"She's ten."

Without hesitation, he responded, "Absolutely. We'll take her for as long as she needs."

When G arrived, she was scared and uncertain. She sat at our dining table for an hour, still wearing her backpack and shoes, contemplating whether to run. That first night was tough. She tested boundaries, asking me if I was mad when she tore up a notebook and threw Kleenex around her room. She vandalized a Mother's Day card I had received and scrawled "Meth Head" across it. Then, she asked, "Are you going to send me back like everybody else? I want to go to juvie."

I reassured her: "I'm not sending you back. And no, you don't want to go to juvie."

I stayed up until she finally fell asleep. The next day, she went to Bible camp. When I picked her up, she was a different child—talkative and happy. From that point on, we built a bond. My family embraced her wholeheartedly. She became part of our family.

Although G didn't stay with us as long as we had hoped, her story came full circle. She was eventually reunited with her mother, along with her siblings. For the first time in five years, they celebrated Thanksgiving, Christmas, and New Year's together as a family.

Through my experiences, I've learned that there is always hope. Recovery is possible. We don't know what each day will bring, but we can choose to show love and grace—not just to the children but also to their parents and the difficult circumstances they face.

I often ask myself: How do I want my grandchildren to remember their time with me? I want them to remember blue skies and butterflies. I want them to experience childhood in all its innocence and wonder. And I want every child to have that same chance.

A Love Letter to My CASA Kids

To my CASA kids:

I know that anyone in your situation would feel uncertain about the future. But I want you to know this: you are strong, and you are brave. What you think matters. *How* you feel matters.

In those moments when you don't know what to do or how to feel, remember that brighter days are ahead. Days filled with sunshine, love, and the freedom to be a child. Days when you will not only seek but find blue skies and butterflies.

I love you with all my heart. Even if I can't always tell the judge exactly what you want me to say, I will always advocate for what is best for you—not just to survive but to thrive.

I want you to know that your parents love you, but sometimes love alone isn't enough. And it's okay to love your parents but hate their actions. Remember, you are not defined by their choices. Your future does not have to reflect your past.

I don't know what the future holds, but I know this: I pray for you. I pray that those you meet will respect you, hear you, and encourage your dreams. Never give up. Always look up.

Even in your darkest moments, remember that God is bigger than you, bigger than your problems. He holds you in the palm of His hand. And when you don't know how to pray, just put your hand on your heart and say, "Jesus, I need You."

With all my love,

Traci

Prologue

<u>TODD COUNTY LAW ENFORCEMENT REPORT</u>

INCIDENT: DOMESTIC DISTURBANCE/ASSAULT FAMILY VIOLENCE

DATE/TIME: AUGUST 23, 2019, 1:15 AM

SCENE: 318 WILLOW STREET
VICTIM: HEATHER WINDSONG
SUSPECT: BOBBY LAROUCHE

CASE NUMBER: CN-82319-I

On 8/23/2019, at approximately, 0115 hours I, Sheriff Tom Dobson, was notified by dispatch of a domestic disturbance call located at 318 Willow Street Mission, SD 57555.

Upon arrival, I observed a female and a male arguing in the front yard.

The female was identified as Heather Windsong, and the male as Bobby LaRouche. Upon my arrival, the female ran toward my vehicle, yelling, "He is going to kill me and my son." I instructed her to stop and show me her hands. At that time, I observed Heather had bruising to her face; around her left eye and left temple area as well as around her neck. I also instructed Bobby to stay where he was as I secured Heather in my patrol vehicle. Bobby was yelling profanities at both me and Heather during that time. I then attempted to deescalate the situation with Bobby while I waited for my back up units to arrive. Shortly thereafter, Tribal Officer Raymond Haus arrived at the scene. Officer Haus stayed with Bobby and conducted an interview with him, while I went back to my patrol vehicle to interview Heather. It should be noted that I observed numerous empty or partially empty alcoholic beverage cans and bottles in the front yard as well has what appeared to be containers for household cleaning agents. I also observed that there was a burn pile near the home to the west and I observed there was still smoke coming from that burn pile at that time.

INITIAL INTERVIEW WITH HEATHER WINDSONG:
Heather advised that she had been consuming alcoholic beverages tonight. Heather advised that she had a two-year-old male child (Jackson), but that she didn't know where he was, and that she hadn't seen him "in a long time." Heather indicated that she wanted to go look for her son. I asked Heather if she would provide me with consent to enter the residence to search for her son. Heather advised that she did want me to go look for her son, but that she no longer lived at this residence, and therefore may not have the legal authority to grant me consent to enter the residence. Heather said that she had been involved in a domestic relationship with Bobby and that she and Jackson had recently moved out. Regarding the incident that occurred tonight, Heather said that her and Bobby had not been getting along for a while, but they were going to try to have a fun family night for Jackson. But instead, Bobby invited a bunch of his friends. She ended up falling asleep and Jackson was with her. When she woke up, Jackson was gone. She wanted to find Jackson and leave. Bobby said he didn't want her to leave. When she asked him where Jackson was, he said it didn't matter, because Jackson wouldn't be going with her anyway. Heather said she panicked. Bobby pushed her down on the couch and started 'smacking' her. She saw a look in his eyes. She had seen it before but tonight it scared her.

I left Heather secured in my patrol vehicle upon concluding this interview.

INITIAL INTERVIEW WITH BOBBY LAROUCHE:
Bobby advised that he had also been consuming alcoholic beverages tonight. Bobby appeared to possibly also be under the influence of narcotics during my interview with him. When I asked Bobby if he was possibly under the influence of any drugs or inhalants, Bobby refused to answer. With respect to the incident that occurred tonight between Bobby and Heather, Bobby said the night started out good. He just wanted to show Heather and Jackson a good time since they would be leaving soon. "Then Heather had to go and start flirting with my buddy, Mike. She always knows what she is doing and how I am going to react. She always trying to make me jealous. Ask her. She'll tell you. This is all her fault. But she know I love her."

I then advised Bobby that I wanted to search the residence, only to look for Heather's son, Jackson, to check on his welfare. I asked Bobby if he would be willing to allow me to search the home under this limited scope, and Bobby stated, "Yes. Fuck. Ok. Yes." I asked Bobby if there were any other people in the home and Bobby said there were not. I also asked Bobby if there were going to be any other substances or things in the home that I should be aware of now, and Bobby again refused to answer that question.

Officer Haus then detained Bobby and placed him in the back of his patrol vehicle. Officer Haus and I then searched Bobby's residence.

SEARCH OF RESIDENCE:

During the search of the residence, I observed in plain view, that there were several items of drug paraphernalia strewn about the kitchen and living room. Those items were: bent spoons that appeared to have been used in the use of illegal narcotics, pipes with crystalline substances within that appeared to have been burned and used, various glass jars containing unknown substances that were presumed to be narcotics, and numerous aerosol cans that appeared to have been used for inhalant abuse purposes. There was music coming from the back bedroom, but no signs of Jackson inside the residence.

Officer Haus and I then exited the residence and secured the scene, as I attempted to obtain a search warrant for the property based on my observations within the home of the illegal narcotics, and due to the fact that we were still unable to locate Jackson at that time.

SECOND INTERVIEW WITH HEATHER:

I then interviewed Heather again and asked about the narcotics observed inside the home. Heather advised that she had no idea they were in the home. In fact, when she arrived at the residence, the place was very clean, which was odd. With respect to Jackson, I asked again about her knowledge of Jackson's last location and Heather advised Jackson was with her when she laid down in the back bedroom but was not with her when she woke up. I did advise Heather that considering what they found in the home and her admitting Jackson was there, she would be charged with endangerment of a child. She was very emotional during this questioning. I read her her Miranda rights.

SECOND INTERVIEW WITH BOBBY:

I then interviewed Bobby again with respect to the narcotics and paraphernalia located within his home. Bobby said they were a gift from Heather. He had no idea she was bringing that stuff. None of it was his. With respect to the search for Jackson, I asked Bobby if Jackson had been here tonight, and Bobby said Jackson laid down around 9 pm to go to sleep. He hadn't seen him since then. I then asked Bobby again about the bruising observed on Heather and he advised that they had gotten into a little argument about her trying to make him jealous. I then advised Bobby that he was under arrest for the domestic violence portion of this incident, I read him his Miranda rights and informed him that I was in the process of obtaining a search warrant for his residence regarding the other observations made on the scene.

Once the search warrant was obtained through Tribal Judge Miller, a more careful search was conducted of the scene. During that search I observed what appeared to be more narcotics, various firearms, and a large sum of cash. Those items were photographed and seized. Additionally, I observed a child's sippy cup, children's clothing, stuffed animals, and blankets. It would appear that Jackson definitely was present at this home at some point. However, the child was still not located at that time.

Rosebud Child Protective Services (CPS) was also contacted at that time.

Dispatch then called me to advise that there was a known associate of Bobby LaRouche that lived nearby to the immediate south of Bobby's residence, by the name of Mike Means. I asked for another unit to check by our location and, shortly after, Officer Leroy from Cherry County arrived at the scene. I asked Officer Leroy to secure Heather in his patrol vehicle, take her to the county jail and start her intake process. I then requested he return back to the LaRouche residence to tape it off with crime scene tape. I asked Officer Haus to take Bobby to the county jail to the holding cell, but not process his intake, yet, as I requested Officer Haus to meet me back at the home of Mike Means.

ADDITIONAL CONTACT MADE WITH WITNESS MIKE MEANS:

Once Officer Haus arrived on scene, we made contact at the residence of Mike Means at 50 Church Street, at approximately 0300 hours. Mike answered the door and appeared to have a white powdery substance on his nose and nostrils (appeared to have been using cocaine). I could hear a young child crying in the background. I asked Mike if that was Jackson, Heather's son. Mike advised that it was, and that he had been present with Bobby and Heather at Bobby's residence earlier that night. Mike stated that he, "Didn't like where things were going" between Heather and Bobby, and decided to leave with Jackson to keep Jackson safe and away from the impending violence. I then entered the residence to secure Jackson and, once again, in plain view, I observed a white substance and a pipe on the floor under the coffee table in the living room area of Mike's home. I then found Jackson in a back bedroom. I secured Jackson in my patrol vehicle, while Officer Haus secured Mike Means in the back of his patrol vehicle.

I then sought a second search warrant for the residence of Mike Means based on the plain view observations in his home, to search the residence for narcotics and related items. The particulars of that investigation, the associated search, and evidence seized will be under case number CN-82319-I2 as that narcotics arrest of Mike Means is unrelated to this call involving Bobby, Heather, and Jackson.

I contacted CPS again and was advised that Family Support Specialist (FSS) Charlie Lawrence would be enroute and should arrive at the scene within an hour. I asked that Charlie meet me at the Todd County Jail instead, as I intended to take Jackson there in my patrol vehicle, as Officer Haus transported Mike Means to jail in his patrol vehicle. A representative of the Indian Child Welfare Act (ICWA) was also contacted as required by law.

I made a stop back at the residence of Bobby LaRouche and verified Officer Leroy taped it off before leaving for the evening. I then proceeded to the jail with Jackson.

All evidence has been properly photographed and submitted to the crime lab for safekeeping.

DEPOSITION:
Arrest -Bobby LaRouche - Assault Family Violence; Possession of Controlled Substance, Endangering a Child
Arrest -Heather Windsong - Possession of Controlled Substance; Endangering a Child
Arrest -Mike Means (see case number CN-82319-l2 for further details)

Sheriff Tom Dobson

Todd County Sheriff's Office

Part One

"Let us put our minds together and see what

kind of life we can build for our children"

~ Sitting Bull, Hunkpapa Sioux

Chapter 1

July 2016 (3 years earlier)

The mattress sagged beneath her. The floor heaved and peeled in areas from the humidity. Both the mattress and floor were discolored. Many of the floorboards were missing, creating easy access for any bug or critter trying to find refuge.

She and Bobby had been invited to a party here, and from that night on, it became their refuge. The house offered privacy and secrecy; it had become their sanctuary.

Two years ago, several houses on the reservation flooded. Many families either couldn't afford to fix them or didn't see the need. Eventually, for one reason or another, the houses sat empty. That was the case with this one. The house wasn't truly hers; in fact, it was probably because of that flood that no one ever came back to claim it. When it first arrived on the reservation through the Habitat for Humanity project, it had been a pretty, light blue color. Now, you couldn't even tell what color it had once been.

On the inside, the plaster on the walls was crumbling. The one light bulb that hung in the middle of the room was useless. The electricity had been shut off since early May. And because they had had one last hard freeze that spring, many of the pipes had burst. Bobby was always saying how he was going to help her and fix the house back up, but that never happened.

Now empty beer cans, whiskey bottles, aerosol cans, and needles were scattered everywhere, nestled in amongst trash and various animal droppings. Fragments of a busted mirror and their jagged edges taunted her.

The walls were bare, except the speckles of mold and bug feces that decorated them like wallpaper. The few clothes she owned laid in a pile in the corner. Her dresser had been hauled out and burned at one of the impromptu parties they had had. Her thoughts, like the dust particles in the room, floated around her. She looked up to follow their descent. Her eyes were drawn to the tiny pinholes that shone sunlight through them. The roof leaked here but very little compared to the rest of the house. Thankfully, at this time of year, she didn't need to worry about the roof. It was late afternoon in July, in what many called the desert of South Dakota. No wind, no rain, no air conditioning, no fans. Despite the once yellow, now black fly strips hanging everywhere, attic flies still buzzed around-slow and lethargic, staking their claim.

She looked around the room, taking in the decay, the wretched conditions. The peeling walls, the sagging furniture–it all mirrored what she had become. Once whole, full of promise, healthy, and hopeful; now broken, neglected and slowly fading away.

What has my life become? The disgusted feelings crawled over her skin. *If only I had just a little something to take the edge off.* Instinctively, she started to sob. Deep sobs. She missed her old life, missed the girl who had dreams and could see a future. She missed being healthy, and, of all things, going to church. She jumped up from the mattress to double check her pockets for a forgotten dime of cocaine. *I promise, God, if you help me find one, this will be my last one.* She paced around the room scanning over the garbage that littered the floor, picking up random aerosol cans only to find them empty. *Just one little hit, please!*

Resigned, she dropped to the mattress again, her eyes resting on the brown paper bag that was meant to keep out the harsh sunlight. The bag had come loose, and on this dry, still day, it was as if it were mocking her- reminding her that no matter how hard one tried, some things –once broken– could never be fixed. Just like the door at the front of the house; it wasn't meant to keep her safe. She wasn't worthy enough to be kept safe. *Shouldn't there be a lock and at least a door handle on the door? Who has a house with no lock and no door handle?* She was disgusted with herself, accepting living in this filth, settling for what was the norm here. She didn't want this to be her life, however, familiarity and a sense of home kept bringing her back.

Although when younger, Heather and Bobby experimented with vodka, cleaning agents, and marijuana, cocaine became their drug of choice. But, if Heather was honest with herself, Bobby was her drug. And that addiction fed all the others.

Since she was 10 years old, she worshipped him. They met at church camp, a place that years later some said was a pipeline for sex traffickers. As for Heather, the memories from that camp haunted her. Singing songs around the campfire, swimming in the river, and the games they would play at mealtimes. As they sat around the table each would try to find someone with their elbows on the table. Sure enough, one evening Heather leaned forward only for a brief moment. Bobby was studying her intently. When she caught him looking at her, he yelled, "Heather, Heather, strong and able, get your elbows off the table." Everyone laughed and giggled.

Even back then, they would sneak out of their cabins and meet at the beach along the Missouri River. Bobby would bring his mp3 player and headphones and let Heather listen to songs he would overhear his uncles listening to. Her favorite was "Fire and Rain" by James Taylor. They would write messages in the sand and build sandcastles on the beach until sunrise. She could hear Bobby's laugh as he chased her with a bullfrog, weaving in and out of the meadow and back down to the beach.

She loved closing her eyes and visiting those times. It wouldn't take long and she would be thinking about the way he would love her. It started out so innocently. They were dared to kiss each other at a junior high party. They drew the shortest straws and so they had to kiss in the dark closet. Before she had anytime to be nervous, he kissed her on her cheek and asked in a hushed whisper if she would want to be his girlfriend. Before she had time to answer, the door was flung open and their friends were giggling and laughing.

From that point forward, he was all she thought about. They eventually went from kissing on the cheek and holding hands to sneaking condoms and beer from his brothers. They were way too young when they first had sex and yet, it seemed so natural. She was adamant about not getting pregnant. She didn't want to be like so many of the teenagers in her high school, either having babies or abortions. It wasn't until they started experimenting with the drugs that they began to lose control.

And the vicious cycle began. One bad decision after another. Bobby had quit school as a sophomore. Once his grandfather died, he became a different person. He spent some time in the Juvenile Detention Center and every time he came home it was like their tragic love story started all over again. It would be a great testament of her loyalty if she could find him a ride from juvie. It wasn't easy and would often times require actions she would never admit to anyone. Bobby didn't care what she had to do as long as he could get back to the rez. And if she did more than what was expected, she could often score some cocaine as a special welcome home treat.

His favorite snacks would be stocked in the cupboard, Budweiser in the refrigerator, and menthol cigarettes and cocaine tucked back in the freezer. The moment he walked in the door, he would pick her up and swing her around. They would proclaim their love for one another and spend the first several days alone, high, and making love. And then, no matter how hard she tried not to; she would end up saying something that would set him off. Something like, "For a long time, I have loved you."

"And?" Bobby would get this look in his eyes and would start to shake.

"And, you have loved me for a long time?" Heather would try to imagine what it was he wanted to hear.

"No, what you were going to say was, you have wasted your life loving me." Heather knew no matter what she said at this point, it was futile. He had gone into his head. He was a tortured soul and no matter how Heather wanted it to be different for him, she didn't know how or what to do. She braced herself for what was going to come.

Heather was an only child, unusual for her Lakota culture, she didn't have a big family. Heather had limited memories of her parents and, for many years, Aunt Neen never talked about them. Later, she was told her dad had died in a head-on collision caused by a drunk driver and her mom of an overdose. Both deaths happened in the same year, when Heather was six years old. Since then, she had lived with her Aunt Neen. *Aunt Neen is the best part of the reservation. She is my home.* Heather experienced unconditional love from her aunt, as if she were her own daughter. Thinking of her aunt and everything she had put her through, she screamed into the empty room, "How did I let this happen? Why can't I change?"

She was brought back to the present, hearing the familiar sound of a startled rodent running underneath the floorboards. There had once been a day when she hadn't been able to sleep knowing there were critters lurking. Now Heather found the sound familiar, she was comforted by the fact that she wasn't alone.

Subconsciously, she hit flies off her arms. As she did so, her fingers felt the sweat pooling on her skin. Her clothes were sticking to her. *Wouldn't I feel better if I just had a hit of something?* She picked up a piece of the jagged mirror. She didn't recognize herself. Her once beautiful, long hair was now chopped to different lengths. She was too thin, and she couldn't tell if the twitching she felt was only in her head. She had an awful, metallic taste in her mouth and her throat was dry. *Just a little something to take the edge off. Then I could think clearly.*

Her life had become like the raging Missouri River; beautiful, strong, and roaring like a lion; but left unchecked, could destroy everything in its path. She already knew how the story would go, only because she'd written it a thousand times before.

Bobby would be 'away' in jail. She would find a job, would feel strong and confident for the first couple of weeks, and would prom-ise herself this time would be different. Yet, the minute she had a paycheck in her hand, every promise would go out the window. Eventually, she would be fired for not showing up or showing up high or drunk. She would fall into the same trap as so many of her people. She would become comfortable with living in poverty.

The sour smell of sickness, dead animals, and garbage overtook her. Rage and disappointment battled within her. Nausea revolted through her and she battled with the familiar itch to get high.

She held the jagged piece of mirror, blood seeped somewhere from the fragmented piece. A beam of sunlight slowly drenched the room in a bright glow. Heather wiped her tears, threw the jagged piece of mirror to the floor and reached for the pregnancy test that lay among the trash. She slowly turned it over, clutched it with both hands and pulled it to her chest, feeling hot tears, once again, roll down her cheeks.

Chapter 2

July 2016

When Heather had come to the door, Neen tried to contain her surprise. Heather had cut her hair. Her jean shorts hung at her hips. Her bones protruded underneath her spaghetti straps. Her eyes were hollow, haunted.

"Hoksichanlkiyapi[1], where have you been? It has been a month! I have been worried!" Aunt Neen moved the wicker basket from the couch and sat down.

Seeing the wicker basket, a chill ran down Heather's spine. The night prior, in a dream, a beautiful woman clothed in a bright native dress and with beads around her head came to her. She had a wicker basket and offered it to Heather. Expecting to see a baby, Heather investigated the basket, but instead a red-purple heart laid inside. She yearned to hold it in her hands. Heather reached in and just as she went to grab it, the basket moved just out of reach. Heather felt a pull to follow the basket. The woman faded away, and suddenly Heather found herself holding the basket. The basket was wet; full of tears. She suddenly heard a squall come from her arms. The basket turned into a beautiful baby. She woke to find the text from her Auntie.

Now, standing here, Heather didn't know where to start. She knew her aunt would be disappointed, but these burdens had become too heavy for her to bear. Aunt Neen had been calling and texting Heather several times a day for the past month. Seeing

---

1   Beloved Child

Heather now, Neen knew something had happened. "Did you feel sorry for me, knowing I was stuck here on such a beautiful day doing laundry?" Neen had been told by some of her friends that Heather hadn't been seen out lately. Sadly, she wasn't showing up for work, but she hadn't been seen at parties either. It was when Bobby started calling and asking about Heather that Neen started to worry. Not at all expecting a response, Neen sent an overly dramatic text earlier in the morning saying she was being buried in clothes and asked Heather if she could bring over another basket. She didn't need a basket, but she did need to know her niecie was safe. It worked. Shortly after, Heather was at her front door with no basket, but an armful of dirty laundry.

Heather grabbed a shirt to fold. As she did so, her mind went to the life in her tummy and how she would be folding little clothes soon.

She laid the shirt down. "Auntie, I'm going to have a baby." Before she chickened out, she hurried through everything. "It's Bobby's, but I haven't told him yet and I don't know where he is. I need to get away from him and that house. I need to get healthy." Before she finished, her voice cracked, "I need to get clean."

Aunt Neen was not naïve to the ways of the young people. She had seen the changes in her dear niecie and, once again, questioned herself about why she didn't leave the reservation so many years ago when she had the chance. The next generation would now face the same struggles she had. Aunt Neen showed none of these doubts on her face. Instead, she grabbed Heather's hand and said, "Have you been to a doctor?"

"No, not yet. I'm scared to go."

"Why are you scared? Are they going to find drugs?" Neen needed to know exactly what they were dealing with.

"Yes. I think so. But I haven't used for over a month. Will it still be in my system?"

"So, you haven't used anything in over a month? You need to tell me. You need to be completely honest with me."

"I have smoked some weed and that's it."

Neen remained silent, knowing the silence sometimes initiated the truth more than asking.

"I can't really remember the last time I did anything else. Maybe two weeks... maybe a week. I'm not sure. I have cravings yet, and that scares me."

"Can you guess how far along you are?"

"I think I'm two months. Will it still be in my system? Have I hurt the baby?"

"There is a very good chance the baby is affected. We'll wait one more month before going to the doctor. For now, we'll go see Elder Miller. He may tell us we need to wait longer. You will move in here immediately. I want you to leave anything you have at that house. We will go to the Goodwill in Yankton first thing in the morning to get clothes and start baby shopping."

Aunt Neen looked past Heather and seemed to be talking to someone other than Heather, "Hoksichanlkiyapi[2,] it is now *our* job to change the direction of *our* story and we look towards wiyohin-pata[3] to begin our climb."

Heather sat completely still, waiting for Aunt Neen to yell or scream, to tell Heather how disappointed she was. Instead, she motioned for her to stand. Aunt Neen pulled Heather into a hug, then stepped back, holding Heather's hands. She looked right at Heather.

"Hoksichanlkiyapi[4], we need to continue to live in gratitude and rely on the strength of family." She pulled Heather back into a hug. As Heather quietly started to cry, Aunt Neen, just as she had done since Heather was a little girl, whispered into her ear, "Shh now, Auntie is here, Auntie is here."

2　Beloved Child

3　The east

4　Beloved Child

Aunt Neen was no stranger to what needed to happen. She was very clear with Heather, "Immediately, you will enroll in AA. You will ask Elder Miller to be your sponsor."

"Why can't you be my sponsor?"

"Because, I haven't been addicted to drugs. I've only been a witness to the damage they cause. You need someone who has been through it. If this doesn't work; you attending meetings and by your own will, then we go to the next step of locking you in your room."

Heather laughed incredulously, "You're not serious."

"Oh, I'm very serious. My ways may not be traditional, but they work. This may require going several days without food or drink. I'm telling you right now, if I think you are tempted, and I will know, and Elder Miller will know, we will get you in that room so fast it will make your head spin. I will not open it under any circumstances, until I'm sure the last of the drugs are out of your system."

Aunt Neen had told her of situations in the past when they had tried this before. It sounded horrific but it usually worked. The last attempt would be tying her to the bed. Aunt Neen said she only saw that happen one time, it was tried only after the user tried jumping out of a second story window to get drugs. Aunt Neen said that that was the only case where she knew the person eventually died of a drug overdose. He couldn't relinquish the demon. Heather wasn't sure if she believed Aunt Neen or not, but she didn't want to find out.

The next day, Heather woke up to the mouthwatering smell of cinnamon rolls and coffee. Checking her phone, she decided to leave her pajamas on for a while. Being that she was up early, she had time to relax for a little bit. Aunt Neen had put up a card table and was sitting at it putting a puzzle together.

Although the first thing Neen did when she woke up was make

sure Heather was still sleeping in her bed, seeing her walk out to the living room, Neen took a deep breath. The fact that Heather didn't leave in the middle of the night gave her hope for their future.

Neen jumped up, "Sit. I will grab you some coffee. We can have rolls here in a little bit." When she was little, one of Heather's favorite things to do was puzzles. She sat at the card table and started sorting pieces.

"Auntie, did you put lavender on the sheets? They smelled so good. I didn't want to get out of bed this morning."

Aunt Neen set a cup of coffee down on the table and went back into the kitchen. "Yes. The quilting girls reminded me how soothing that smell can be if done just right. So, I can report back to them, I did good?" She walked back in with the rolls and napkins.

Heather laughed a little, "Yes. Tell them you did good." Heather continued to rearrange puzzle pieces. Without looking up, she said, "I would like to go this morning to see Elder Miller, but I should get a new number first so I can give it to him. Would you call him and see if he is available?"

"I can, but what do you think of me going with you?" Aunt Neen slid a roll in front of Heather. It smelled so good, but Heather was afraid she may throw it up if she ate it. She took a small bite. *Of course, Auntie wants to come with me. She doesn't trust me. Who am I kidding? I don't trust myself.*

"Yes, of course you can come with me. That's probably a good idea."

When Aunt Neen called Elder Miller, he was in his garden. When Aunt Neen asked if he had time to meet later that morning, he simply said, "Yes. Meet me here."

They drove the few miles to the cell phone store and obtained a new phone number for Heather. They then drove to Elder Miller's. Growing up, Heather had heard stories about Elder Miller's house, but she hadn't really paid any attention until now. It sat on the campus of the college. Strangely, it looked both out of place and yet stood majestically proclaiming it's birthright. It was massive, with two stories and a wraparound porch. There were pillars on the front that stood guard as if determined to hold the house up. The overhang to the porch was sagging, the porch floor was heaving, but you could tell, back in its day, it was considered majestic.

Noticing the way Heather looked at the house, Aunt Neen explained, "Back in the 1800's there was a battle amongst our people and the white man over the discovery of gold in the Black Hills. Elder Miller's Great Grandpa saved the little boy of a white man from drowning in the Niobrara River. The white man had built this house thinking that this is where the railroad would run through. Once the war was over and our people were moved here, the railroad had moved to Valentine. The white man, having already decided to move with the railroad, in great grandeur, gifted the house to Chief Millhawk, Elder Miller's Great Grandpa. However, there was one condition to our tribe receiving the house and that was Chief Millhawk had to change his name to Miller. Back then, the white man had strange demands on our people. Much of which we still don't understand today. But, through the years, this house has served as a reminder of what can be lost in war and what can be gained. It has held magic in it. People come here to be healed."

Today, Heather wore a sundress she had found buried in the back of the closet. She wanted what she wore to imitate what she was feeling on the inside. A new start, a positive, bright future. She found a blue jean jacket and put that on as well. She wasn't ready to show off her track filled arms quite yet. The dress had big pockets in the front. As they walked around back, Heather dug her hands into them.

She was surprised to see nothing but beautiful flowers; vibrant colors, differing heights, and varying sizes. Some with big bulbs that cascaded down the stems and others with small bursts of seeds sprouting from the middle of velvet leaves. There was a white picket fence that needed new paint and, despite its best efforts, it was clear it could not contain the entire garden. It had two sides that wrapped around, leaving the front of the garden open. Heather allowed herself to imagine what it was like so many years ago, when this probably sat like so many of the dry, vacant lots. *The myth that nothing can grow from these lands is definitely proven wrong here. How wonderful it must be to have been the one to watch these beautiful creations grow.* Heather felt a force pulling her forward. She reached out to touch the velvet petal. Suddenly she remembered why she was there and her hands quickly went back into her pockets.

"Hello?" Aunt Neen, being here several times before, walked around to the west side. Heather slowed her steps and took in the fragrant smells that embraced her. "Heather, come on. We're around back." Heather walked towards Neen's voice and found both Elder Miller and Auntie sitting on a bench.

Heather walked over to sit. Aunt Neen slid away from Elder Miller so Heather had no choice but to sit between them. Heather cleared her voice and began to speak, "I need –"

"Speak up child. These ears aren't what they used to be." Elder Miller and Aunt Need passed a glance between them. Heather tried again, mustering the confidence she did not feel. He agreed to meet with her once every week. From that first meeting, and every time after, he would end the conversation whispering the most comforting words, "Peace, sister."

At the end of September, Elder Miller's best guess was that she was roughly three months along. Once he was satisfied Heather was doing the work needed, he recommended a doctor in Valentine. Right around the start of October, Heather could start to feel the baby kick.

It was at her 20-week checkup, Dr. Kneip put her on prenatal vitamins and conducted a detailed ultrasound. She explained to Heather and Aunt Neen that if all went well, the ultrasound would show the baby's organs, limbs, and any potential developmental issues. Heather was filled with anxiety for the next several days until the doctor called and said the baby looked perfectly healthy.

Heather wouldn't say it out loud, and although she was resolute in her decision, there were times where she missed Bobby terribly. *If he could feel the baby kick, would it make him think differently?* She hadn't talked to Bobby since she left. He had tried calling Aunt Neen a couple of times, but one mention to Elder Miller about the unwanted phone calls and they soon stopped.

Going into December, and her third trimester, it was one of the coldest winters they had seen in a while on the reservation. Heather was thankful she was with her Aunt Neen. If she was still with Bobby, she would be in a freezing, run down shack, strung out just so she could forget where she was and what she was doing to herself.

Heather had been doing everything Aunt Neen told her. She not only cut all communication with Bobby, but with all of her old friends as well. The one friend she did have, Lola, had moved off the reservation and was going to college in Mitchell. Lola had called Heather a couple of times to check in, usually asking about the pregnancy, Aunt Neen, and whether or not she had been in contact with Bobby. She was the only one outside of her aunt, Elder Miller, and her doctor that had Heather's new phone number. Heather appreciated Lola thinking about her. When Heather told her about starting AA, Lola mentioned Mitchell had a great AA program as well. She suggested that maybe Heather could come visit at some point.

With all of the new changes, Heather had good days and bad days. On the days she was feeling anxious, she would bundle up and walk to the Missing and Murdered Indigenous Women (MMIW) office to see her Aunt Neen. She learned how to see the symptoms coming and would tell herself to give it a little bit, she would soon feel better. Heather had more good days than bad and for that she was thankful. Her favorite time of day was early in the morning. She would get up early, make hot tea, and do the Suduko puzzle or just scroll on her phone. She was feeling like her old self, the old self before the drugs. Aunt Neen was constantly there, physically when she was nauseous and emotionally, when the old feelings started to creep in. Heather would be invited to attend quilting with her aunt and down to the Community Center on Saturdays for game day. She had to admit, she looked forward to Neen's friends asking about the baby and always asking if they could feel the baby kick. Neen also attended church every Sunday and always invited Heather. Heather was feeling the pull, but couldn't bring herself to attend yet.

They had just gotten home from the grocery store and it was unusually nice out for December, so they decided to go for a walk. Heather vocalized her apprehension for the future. Again, Aunt Neen reminded Heather she was a beautiful, strong Ina.[5] The first time Aunt Neen called Heather Ina; she was 12 years old. She still remembered how Aunt Neen explained that Ina meant several things. It encompassed the first of everything, first connection to the world, first source of nourishment, first bond, first healer, first friend. From that moment, Aunt Neen loved teaching Heather her native language of Lakota, and Heather loved learning it. Somehow, it made her feel more connected to her parents who had moved on to the Spirit World and then, later, more connected to Bobby.

Ina. Since Heather became pregnant, she had thought a lot about that name. She thought about the circle of life and how the word was reciprocal. Reciprocal between her and her Auntie and soon between her and her baby. It was the circle of life. And she was so grateful to be clean to experience every part of it. It was during this discussion, while on their walk, when Heather asked, "Auntie, what would you think about me going to Mitchell to visit Lola?"

"I would be worried. Do you think you're ready?"

"Honestly? I'm not sure. Would you want to go with me?"

---

5 Mother

"Yes, I think so. Maybe we could do some shopping for the baby while we're there?"

"Could we visit the college?" The words rushed from Heather's mouth as if she had no control of them.

Aunt Neen's heart was soaring. She knew she needed to be very careful as to how she reacted. She had prayed for this for so long.

"Of course, Ina. Are you thinking of going to school?"

"Yeah. I am. But, how would it work with you still here?"

"What do you mean, child?"

"What I mean is, I have heard about the awful time our people can have when a family member leaves the reservation. Lola has told me how her family now refers to her as Apple. They no longer call her by her name. I would also be worried about you here, without me."

Neen had not considered that she could be the reason Heather would stay.

"Do you know why they call her Apple?"

"Yes. Because she has left the reservation, she is still red on the outside but white on the inside." Heather stopped and looked at Aunt Neen, "Would they let me come back and visit? We need you in our life." Heather's hands went to her tummy.

Neen couldn't believe they were having this conversation in 2016. This was the same conversation they were having 30 years ago. *What is holding our people back?* It was a question she, herself had struggled to answer her whole life. She had witnessed first-hand the mental anguish her people wrestled with. The pull to leave but the obligation to stay.

They had just reached the playground area of the grade school. A colorful bench beckoned them. Once they were both seated, Neen looked right at Heather. "What is the most beautiful part of the apple?" Aunt Neen didn't wait for an answer. "The outside. The red. Same with us! Do you know that the color red is a sign of strength and power? Did you know we are calling on the color red to make us visible again?"

Aunt Neen was referring to the work she was doing with MMIW. "I will always be in your life. Whether that is here or in Mitchell. No one will stop that from happening, ever. I am going to ask you to do something. Will you think only about your future and the future of your baby? Leave our ancestors out of it, leave Bobby out of it, and leave me out of it."

"But–" Heather didn't want to leave Aunt Neen out of anything.

"No, Ina, my child, listen to me. I know you feel an obligation to our land, to our culture, to our people, to stay. Our ways of life have not kept up to the forward thinking of our young people. The time is now that we must encourage a new way of thinking, of living. We, together with the white man, must change the future for the better of our people, our children. Yes, we want to see change. That cannot happen if we are living in the past. If we decide to respect each other's cultures, that will transcend the past. I don't want you to just survive. More than anything, I want you to dream, to set goals and, more importantly, give your child the opportunities I wasn't able to give to you. If all of this is only possible by learning how to work with the white man, then so be it. Let us change the meaning of Apple. Let us work together to change the ways of our people. Rather than look at the apple as just red and white, let's focus on the seeds of the apple. Your baby. The future of what is to come. Our children. Only our children." Neen grew silent, lost in her own thoughts.

Heather changed the subject. "I loved growing up here, Auntie, but I also know, as an adult, I need to find my own way. My sobriety has got to be my focus. The reservation doesn't help me with that. I was so worried about the past; my future began to fade. I don't want to go back to that. I have too much at stake." Heather once again rubbed the bump protruding from her belly.

Neen's voice dropped to a whisper, "The creator gifted you to me so many years ago and now we have grown up together. In this world, you are my child. In the spirit world you are also my Ina, *my* teacher, *my* whole world. My heart beats in you and our hearts will beat in this little one." She closed her eyes, "No matter where we are; in this world or the spirit world, that will never change." After a brief pause, Neen lifted her head. "And so, yes, we will go to Mitchell and see your friend!" She stood up, reached for Heather's hand and said, "Come. Let's go get your future."

Chapter 3

April 2017

Heather's last trimester was filled with doctor's appointments and getting the house ready for baby. Between feeling the baby kick, the vivid dreaming, and the constant need to pee, Heather wasn't getting much sleep at night. She was going to weekly doctor's appointments and they talked extensively with her doctor about not using certain narcotics for pain meds during and after delivery. Her doctor also reminded her how important it would be for her to stay away from the drug scene once she had the baby. "Now, you are focused on this baby. Your body has changed and you are a different person when you're carrying a child. After you have the baby and you start feeling like your old self is when you need to be extra careful." Heather was listening, but she also knew she was done with that part of her life. She would have a baby to take care of and love.

With the help of the prenatal vitamins, Heather's hair was black, thick, and hung to the middle of her back. Her face radiated with the 'baby glow' she had heard about. She had started going to church a while back and she lined up a job at McDonald's that she would start shortly after having the baby. She couldn't wait for her future. She couldn't wait to be a mom.

Heather's water broke in the middle of the night on April 21st, 2017, exactly one week past her due date. They thought they had plenty of time to get to the hospital in Valentine as she was suffering with low, dull back pain but contractions were still 10 minutes apart. It was when they pulled up to the ER door that Heather started holding her breath, anticipating the sharp stabs of pain that would start in her lower back and roll around to her abdomen. Just before the nurse opened the door, Aunt Neen grabbed Heather's hand, "Breathe, Ina, baby is coming soon."

Neen had called the hospital before they left, letting them know they were coming from Mission and would be there within 40 minutes. There were two nurses waiting for them, one with a wheelchair and the other with what looked like an upright mini desk on wheels. With intention but with focus, the nurse came around to Heather's side of the car and helped her into the wheelchair. The other nurse started asking Heather and Neen questions, everything from what Heather had eaten that night to how far apart her contractions were.

Once they arrived at the room there were another two nurses waiting for them. They all had their role to play. One was on the phone with the doctor. One was hooking Heather up to oxygen and putting a bracelet on her. The other was prepping the warming table for baby. The last nurse, who was the one that pushed Heather's wheelchair up to her room, helped Heather climb into bed.

She smiled at Heather, introducing herself, "Hi, Heather. My name is Tara and I am going to help you deliver this beautiful baby!" She looked at Heather's chart. "I'm seeing that this is your first baby. And we do not want to do any narcotics. But I want you to know the epidural is still an option. So, you need to let me know as we get going if that is something you would like. Once the contractions start coming consistently, you will pull your knees up to your chest, take a big breath, and push." She looked to Aunt Neen, "While Heather is pushing, Neen, you'll be counting from 1 to 10. We'll be watching the monitor. As we see the next contraction coming, we'll ask you to take that big deep breath and pretend you are pushing a deep growl into your stomach. Instead of yelling or screaming, try to use that for the deep push. We are all here to help, but you have to do the hard work when the time comes, ok? You've *got this.*"

Heather would remember that nurse for many years after, as she looked around the same age as Heather, but seemed so confident in what she did. She had kind eyes and she spoke to Heather in a way that made Heather feel like she was incapable of failing.

The next several hours continued in a blur. Heather decided to forego the epidural as hard contractions started four hours after they arrived. The last thing Heather remembered was Tara showing Aunt Neen where to stand while she counted the pushes. For Aunt Neen, so many emotions were rushing through her. She was witnessing, for the first time, a baby being born. She was filled with love and pride for her dear niecie. Heather was doing something Neen never did. The whole experience was a miracle and she thanked her Creator for letting her be a part of it. The doctor asked Aunt Neen if she wanted to cut the umbilical cord. She didn't hesitate.

Jackson came into the world with barely a cry. So much so, that for a moment, Heather held her breath until she heard a gurgle and a collective sigh and then giggles from the nurses that huddled around him.

The nurse laid him on her chest. Heather had read how important it was to have skin to skin contact immediately after the baby was born. *Thank you, God.* Heather cried. Aunt Neen cried. Jackson quieted and slept. Heather knew being a mother was her sole purpose. It was confirmed by the soft skin, pouty lips, and the darkest, longest eyelashes she had ever seen. Heather could physically feel the bond being formed. *Is this what my mother experienced when she had me?*

"Do we have a name for baby?" The nurse asked in a hushed tone. Heather looked at Aunt Neen. "Yes, we are naming him after my dad: Jackson Bear Robe Windsong." The nurse wrapped a bracelet around Heather's wrist and did the same for Jackson.

Aunt Neen laid her hand on the baby's back and whispered. "Happy Birthday, baby." She took Heather's hand and whispered, "I am so proud of you, Ina. You are going to be the best mommy."

Heather continued to let the tears fall. For the next hour, there was the hustle and bustle of trying to get Jackson to suckle from her breasts and having Heather eat a little something. After bringing Jackson from being weighed, Heather had fallen asleep and so Neen gladly took him from the nurse, sunk into the recliner next to Heather's bed, and snuggled him.

While Heather slept, the nurse brought in a bouquet of blue carnations and a balloon that said "It's a Boy!" There was no card. Neen assumed they were from Lola as she had tried calling Heather's phone while she slept.

They left the hospital two days later. The Pasque flower was just beginning to emerge and the lilac trees were in full bloom. Throughout the summer of 2017, Heather settled into mom life. She was expecting to feel some postpartum depression as her doctor warned her of the symptoms, however, so far, she hadn't felt anything other than gratitude for a second chance.

One month after having the baby, Heather started working at McDonald's in Winner. Her and Jackson made their home with Aunt Neen. Because Aunt Neen was no longer working, she continued to fill her time volunteering for the Missing and Murdered Indigenous Women (MMIW). And because that was part time, she assured Heather it made sense for her to watch Jackson while Heather was at work.

Neen had a way of helping and yet not overstepping. The three of them would go for long walks and Neen would take these opportunities to talk to Heather. She would tell Heather stories about when she was a young girl. She would remind Heather that past behaviors are in the past. And so, it is ok to look forward and dream of a bright future. Aunt Neen was always vague when talking about her past as a young girl. Heather knew there was something she wasn't saying.

Neen continued to encourage Heather to attend school off the reservation. Ever since they took the trip to Mitchell to visit Lola, Heather had been giving it a lot of thought. Aunt Neen wanted Heather to experience the campus again with nicer weather and with Jackson. A doctor's appointment in Mitchell for Aunt Neen allowed the perfect excuse to go. In late June, with a two-month-old in tow, they drove to Mitchell.

The campus was surrounded with lush green grass and majestic brick buildings. Beautiful, vibrant plants exploded from big, clay pots. A walking path that wrapped around campus invited long conversations and reflection as well as walking and running. Heather couldn't wait to try it out. Both with Jackson in the stroller and as a moment of meditation for herself. She allowed herself to feel the pull this place was having on her. If she were to vocalize what she was feeling, Aunt Neen would tell her it was her ancestors guiding her. Heather decided not to say anything just yet.

While on campus this time, they met with the nursing instructor and talked about scholarships and financial aid. Lola had gone with them on the visit and made sure to take them to the chapel on campus. Neen loved seeing this side of Heather. The younger version that could laugh with her friend. She knew Heather would thrive here, but Neen also knew it needed to be Heather's decision.

Lola had done research on open apartments in the same complex as her, as well as the daycare on campus. She knew there was availability in both. Lola made the comment in her very cheery voice, "It's as if this is meant to be!" Aunt Neen was thinking the exact same thing. She knew Heather's dream was to be a nurse and she couldn't get that degree if she stayed. Neen asked Heather if she would consider enrolling in August, promising she would come visit every weekend. Heather assured her Auntie she would think about it.

Following the campus visit, they grabbed lunch and then headed to Aunt Neen's doctor's appointment. Aunt Neen was adamant that Heather stay in the car so as to not disrupt a sleeping Jackson.

When Heather pressed Aunt Neen as to what the doctor said; Neen waved it off and said she would know more in a couple of days.

August came with big changes. As Heather graduated from the 12-step program, she heard Bobby had gotten in trouble again and would be going away for several years. She was more determined than ever to follow her own path and make a sustainable life for her and Jack. She applied and was accepted into the college in Mitchell and would start right away in September.

This required her to start planning and moving immediately. Upon verifying the apartment was still available and that there was an opening for Jack at the daycare, she called Lola and gave her the good news. Aunt Neen could hear Lola squeal on the other end. A rush of sadness came over Neen. She pushed it down and instead said, "Ina, let me keep Jack for a couple of weeks while you settle into your apartment and into a routine."

Heather conceded. "Ok. But as soon as I get settled, I want you and Jack down there ASAP."

Once Heather arrived in Mitchell, she got busy, so busy she barely had time to check in with Aunt Neen. She made appointments for her financial and utility assistance. She met with her social worker and set up well checks for Jack. At night, her and Lola were exploring Mitchell, playing pool and darts, and just hanging out at the local bars. Lola had a fake ID and mentioned to Heather a couple of times that she could get her one. Heather was adamant it wasn't necessary, since she didn't drink. Heather had to admit, there were times when she had to really talk herself out of taking a sip. She knew she needed to have a talk with Lola about not going out as much. Heather was becoming increasingly comfortable in the bar setting and she knew it wasn't good for her finances or her mental health. And she didn't have the accountability she had when Aunt Neen and Jack were around.

Her first week in Mitchell, Heather planned various meetings with different departments at the college. First, she met with her advisor and went through her class schedule. Her advisor mentioned doing work study as a part time job, she was excited to look into that.

Her next stop was Financial Aid. The office housed a desk with two chairs in front of it and a table off to the side. An apricot smell floated through the air, she couldn't decide if she liked it or not. Just as Heather was about to sit down, a plump, curly-haired, middle-aged woman came around the corner and said, "Let's move to the table." Once they were seated, the lady looked at her above her glasses. "I don't believe we have met. You are?" Instantly, Heather's guard went up.

"I am Heather Windsong. We met briefly a couple of weeks ago when my Auntie and I came and toured." Her voice spoke confidence she wasn't feeling.

"And, how can I help you?" Heather wasn't sure how to respond. *Didn't she know I was coming in?* "Well – I – uh – my advisor said you were on my schedule for today?"

"Ok. But do you know why you are here, in this office? Do you know what it is I do?"

Heather was afraid she was going to say the wrong thing. She must have paused a little too long because Carol (according to her name plate on the desk) continued, "How are you going to pay for your classes?"

Heather shifted in her chair. "Well, I plan to get a job and doing work study."

"Ok. And you have a son? Who will be taking care of him while you are at class and work study?"

"I have daycare lined up right close here to campus."

"And who is paying for daycare?" Heather was getting the impression Carol didn't believe a word she said. *I will prove you wrong, you just wait and see.*

"I will. I will have some assistance. My Auntie is going to help in any way she can, as well."

"Ok. My job is to help you figure out a way to graduate with a degree while going into the least amount of debt possible. This requires us to look at all of your finances, not just school. If you allow me, I will help you budget and save. We will start building your legacy right here, right now. My name is Carol. Let's get down to business." She looked right at Heather and smiled. Carol instantly turned from a scary white woman to a sweet grandma.

After going through the checklist and talking through the paperwork, Carol encouraged Heather to provide them with her membership card to the tribe. "There will be some assistance there and why not get all the help we can?"

Heather nodded in agreement. "Do you mind if I send a text right now to my Auntie to see if she has that?" Shortly after sending the text, Heather's phone pinged. "Auntie is going to call the office right now and request a copy be faxed directly here."

"Perfect. I will go out and let the girls know to look for it." It couldn't have been more than five minutes when Heather's phone pinged again.

It was a text from a blocked caller that simply read, "Really? Mitchell?" *Whose number is this? Other than Auntie and Lola, who knows I am here?*

Carol had just walked back into the office, "Got it!"

"Ok - Let's put this number..." Carol was talking, but Heather was only half listening.

Heather's phone pinged again. It was from Auntie, "They said they were going to fax right away. Did you receive it?" She sent Neen a quick message back.

Her phone pinged again. It was a blank message from the same blocked number. The hair on Heathers neck stood up. It wasn't the fact that she was receiving messages from a blocked number. What bothered her was, except for the people at school, no one had this number. She put her phone on silent and tried to concentrate on what Carol was saying.

Chapter 4

October 2017

Heather had put this conversation off for as long as she could. There was no better time than now. She hadn't been home for two weeks and had only talked to Aunt Neen maybe three times since she left. Aunt Neen was not surprised when Heather finally did call and said she needed to talk and she wanted to do so in person. Neen asked Heather to meet her at the Dollar Store in Winner before they would continue to Mission. The October day was cold and frigid.

"Where is your coat?" Neen asked Heather the minute she stepped into the store.

"I can't find it. It isn't too bad out. Where's Jack?"

"He's at home. The neighbor kids came over for a while to watch him. I didn't want to take him out in this cold. And I thought this would give us an opportunity to pick up some things while being able to talk in private."

"OK. I can't wait to see him." The words fell flat. Heather grabbed a cart and moved off to the side, allowing Aunt Neen to push from one side, while Heather still had her hand on it. They had been shopping like this ever since Heather came to live with Aunt Neen 14 years ago. And one of their favorite places to shop was the Dollar Store.

"How are things going?" Aunt Neen asked, slowly guiding the cart down the aisle. "I see you have your hair and nails done–very pretty. Have you received any more phone calls?"

"Not since that day in the Financial Aid office. But, Auntie, Carol from the FA office said she hasn't received the monies from the tribe. What is going on?"

Aunt Neen lowered her voice, "They are being assholes! I've been there twice and they say they will send it. I am going to call a friend of mine that works at the university here. His name is Simon White Eagle. He is a good man. He believes in education. I think he will help us."

Heather was about to bring up the difficult conversation she wanted to have when Aunt Neen continued, "I am worried about someone being in contact with Bobby. Are you thinking the blocked calls came from him?"

"Yes, I don't know who else it would be? I also received those flowers at the hospital. I thought they were from Lola, but she said she didn't send them." Heather reached for a can of tomato soup. Aunt Neen handed her a piece of paper and a pen. No words needed to be spoken. Again, Heather was always in charge of crossing items off as they picked them up.

"We can get you a new number. I think we should do that." Heather had come home for the weekend and it took everything she had to come back. Yes, she wanted to see Aunt Neen and of course, Jack, but she also had a life now, in Mitchell.

"I don't want to get a new number. Something as simple as my phone number, he wants to take. I won't let him. I changed it already once before and everyone at the school has this one." *And all of my friends.* "I just don't understand how it's possible. If he's in jail, how were they able to tell him right then that I was in Mitchell? It honestly scares me. Does he have someone watching us? And I'm worried for you and Jack, here."

"Jack and I are just fine!"

Heather used this as her opportunity to talk to Aunt Neen about why she came home. "Are you sure? Because, Auntie, what do you think about Jack staying with you longer? I'm worried about having Jack in Mitchell when I can't be with him."

"What do you mean? You can't be with him?"

"When I'm at school and work then he needs to be at daycare. I'm worried Bobby will somehow get to him." Heather knew she was exaggerating, but she needed Aunt Neen to say yes to keeping him. She was just getting settled and meeting new people. She didn't want to be stuck home with Jack when Lola and everyone else were going out and having fun.

"How is your sobriety going?"

"It's going good."

"How is Lola doing?"

"Why are you asking me all of these questions? I just asked if Jack could stay a little longer. It's no big deal."

"Yes, yes, it is a big deal. First of all, I am not asking a lot of questions. I am trying to figure out what your head space is. I love Jack, but he is *your* son, Ina. Just curious, how long are you thinking you want him to stay with me?"

"Just forget it. Forget I asked. Are we about done, so I can go see Jack?"

When they arrived home, Jack was sitting with one of the neighbor girls reading his favorite puppy book.

Heather put the bags of groceries on the countertop. She went to Jack and picked him up. He felt foreign in her arms. He began to whimper. "Ah, little man, it has only been a few weeks. You remember your momma, don't you?"

Aunt Neen fluttered around, putting groceries away and talking to the babysitter. She handed the girl a couple of dollars, "Tell your mom to come see us one of these days." The girl shook her head yes before she dashed to the door. Aunt Neen gave a little chuckle, wishing she had the energy that young girl did.

"What's so funny?" Listening to the tone in which Heather asked, Aunt Neen knew Heather was not herself.

"Nothing. Just thinking about the energy that young girl has. I wish she could give me some. Do you want me to take him?"

"No, just tell me why he is crying."

"First of all, relax. He can sense your nervous energy. Do you see his bottle, anywhere?

"I already tried his bottle. He didn't want it." Heather talked over Jack's little whimpers. "Just take him."

Aunt Neen reached for Jack and he immediately cuddled into her neck.

"I can only stay tonight. We have pumpkin painting with Lola and her friends tomorrow afternoon." Heather ignored the look of disappointment on Aunt Neen's face. She remembered Aunt Neen asking the last time they talked on the phone if she would want to come home and carve pumpkins and decorate with baby boos and gourdes from the community garden.

"What are your plans for Thanksgiving? When do you start winter break? Did you plan on trick or treating with Jack?" Heather couldn't concentrate. Her mind drifted back to Mitchell, wondering what her friends were doing.

***

The next day, Heather was sitting at the kitchen table making two lists. The first one was everything she needed to do when she got back to Mitchell and the second was a list of expenses she had coming due. "I could really use that money from the tribe."

Aunt Neen was at the sink making tea. "Well, unfortunately, I am not sure when that will come through. I will try calling Simon again at the school and perhaps Elder Miller can help."

Jack was still sleeping. Aunt Neen had turned on the space heater and the house was warm. *Almost too warm.* Normally, Heather would love these slow, relaxed mornings, but today she was having a hard time sitting still. *Why do I feel like I am wasting my time here? I should be back in Mitchell getting stuff done.*

"Do you have time to stay and paint pumpkins?"

Heather quickly sent a text to someone and then threw the phone down on the table. "You're not serious!" Heather laughed. "This is my list of things I need to have done by Monday. I will be up late tonight and tomorrow night trying to get all of this done."

"Well, I am very glad, then, you were able to get a good night's rest last night, since I kept Jack." Although Aunt Neen was trying to sound funny, it came across flat.

Heather's voice went up an octave. "I asked if you wanted me to take him and you didn't answer me." Heather went to the stove to refill her mug with hot water. "I ended up falling asleep. Between work study, regular work, and classes, I'm barely keeping up."

"Would it help if I came up there on the weekends?" Although Aunt Neen was trying to help, Heather could feel herself panic. The last thing she wanted was to have to be tied to her apartment on the weekends by hosting Aunt Neen. She needed her weekends for down time. Those weekends were what helped her get through the week. Heather needed to come up with something.

"What if you guys planned on coming to Mitchell for Halloween? We can plan on Jack staying with me that following week and see how it goes? That way I can focus on getting as much stuff done as I can before then? Speaking of which, I should probably get my stuff put together. Lola was hoping I could make it back in time to go with her to get supplies for the pumpkin painting." Heather didn't wait for a response. She grabbed her to-do list but conveniently left her list of expenses on the table and went to grab her things.

CHAPTER 5

Aunt Neen decided to give Heather one more week of freedom and then enough was enough. On the following Friday she went to see Heather at her work study. The entire way over to Mitchell, Neen was doubting herself, wondering if this was the right thing to do. *I hope she knows how much I love her and this little guy.* She mentally went through the list of concerns she wanted to bring up to Heather. *I want to be understanding, but I also need her to take responsibility.*

"Nana's here, Jackie." With Neen's tender words, the squall coming from the backseat quieted. With those few words of comfort, Neen thought about turning around. *What if he needs me? What if he wonders why I left him? How old do they have to be to understand that type of stuff?* Neen was now talking out loud. "Ok, buddy, I am going to talk to your mom. If it doesn't go good, you will come back home with me, but we aren't going to tell her that. We are going to think positively and we are going to remind her of why she is the best mommy for you."

Heather looked concerned. She quickly jumped up from her desk and greeted Neen at the door, "Here, let me take him. What are you doing here? What's wrong?" Heather grabbed the car seat from Aunt Neen.

Heather quieted an impulse to put some gum in her mouth and to check her appearance. Aunt Neen showing up today was the last thing Heather expected. She sent up a thank you to the Spirit world for making her get her butt into work that morning. She had laid in bed for a half hour wanting to call in sick.

"Is there any chance you can take your break now? Could we go to the bookstore for a coffee?" Neen didn't mind that at this point Heather was very concerned as to why they showed up out of the blue. She was hoping the element of surprise would work for her.

"I don't think it will be a problem. Let me go check with my supervisor."

Heather explained to her supervisor her Auntie was there and it must be important for her to just show up like this.

"She said to take all the time I need. Did you bring the stroller?"

Neen didn't want Heather to see the car packed with all of Jack's things just yet, so she offered to grab it.

Once they clicked the car seat into the stroller and tucked the diaper bag underneath, they made their way to the bookstore. "I'm glad you guys are here, but why are you here?"

"We're here because I need to talk to you. And I need you to listen with an open mind. Let's get our coffees ordered and then we can talk. My treat."

The bookstore was the hub of campus. It was located within the campus library just a few steps from Starbucks. The smell was a mixture of coffee, books, and vanilla. It was bright, clean, and inviting. This was Heather's favorite place on campus. The library was brimming with excitement that day as they were having the Governor of South Dakota in, along with a panel of speakers, to talk about the poverty in South Dakota. Heather was interested in attending, but she had also been invited to play intramural soccer that day.

They walked up to the counter. "Hey girl, what's up?" The barista had purple hair, glasses, and was very animated.

"Not much, my Auntie is in town, so we stopped to grab a drink." As if Jack was reminding Heather he was there, he gave a little squall. "Oh, this is my baby, Jackson."

The barista leaned over the counter to look at Jack, "What? No way! I didn't know you had a kid."

Heather laughed, "Yep! He's my son." *I still can't believe I have a son.* Just as the barista was going to continue the conversation, Heather turned to Aunt Neen, "What do you want to drink? I still have money on my student card. I can get it."

"No, you will not!" Aunt Neen stepped forward. "I will get it and I will have whatever you are having."

Once they put their order in, they found a table that offered some privacy. Aunt Neen quickly made a bottle and propped it so Jack could eat; she wanted to be able to focus on what she was about to say to Heather.

"I think it is time for Jack to come live with you." She blurted the words out.

"Ok, yes, we talked about this. He is going to stay with me for a week after Halloween. Isn't that what we decided?" Heather's heart was beating fast.

"Yes. That is what you talked about but then I don't hear from you for a whole week. I feel like you tell me what I want to hear and not what is really going on. Also, you went to all the work to set up his appointments and get on assistance, you are ready to have him come live with you, aren't you?" Neen was trying to keep her voice steady and calm.

"Fine! Whatever!" Heather could feel herself wanting to cry. And she didn't want to cry here. The purple-haired girl came over to deliver their drinks. "Is there anything else I can get you?" Heather shook her head no, "We're good."

The purple-haired girl looked down at Jack and said, as she turned around, "Cute kid."

Aunt Neen took a sip of her coffee. "Mmm, this is pretty good!"

"I just don't understand what changed from last week to now." Heather was going to try to explain to her Auntie why now may not be the best time. *Especially this week, why would she do this to me?* "I'm not even sure they still have an opening at daycare."

"They do. I called yesterday to double check."

"Are you serious? You called his daycare and they just tell you whatever you ask? Wow, that's good to know."

"I am an emergency contact, am I not?" Neen took a deep breath. "Heather, Jack needs you. He needs to know you. I know you can only see the hard stuff right now, but God has given you such a special privilege. Not everyone gets the chance to be a mom."

"Oh, I see, you think because people like you weren't able to have kids, those of us that can, can no longer have a life of our own? Is that it? I actually knew you would do this."

"Do what?"

"You make decisions and expect everyone to just do what you say. You don't care how it affects anyone else as long as you are happy." *Oh, little girl, if you only knew.* Neen remained quiet.

Heather was filled with rage. "Actually, Jack will be better off with me. He will learn not everything will be handed to him. It will take him a while, but he will forget about living with you. And this way you won't have to worry about anything. Since I don't have any of his things and can't afford anything right now, we will have to make do but, not your problem anymore, right?" Heather smirked and took a drink of her coffee.

Aunt Neen hated it when Heather talked to her like this. She knew Heather wasn't herself. Neen also knew Heather always had been good at using her words as weapons. "Are you tired? Or not feeling well? Why are you talking to me like this? I did bring all of Jack's things with me."

"Wow! You really are just like my mom!" Something in Aunt Neen snapped. She slapped Heather's cheek hard and fast. Tears began to pool in the corners of Heather's dark eyes.

"I am sorry I did that, Ina. But I am *nothing* like your mother."

Heather looked over to the young girl at the counter hoping she didn't notice. The girl looked at her with pity and quickly looked away.

Oh my God, I am so embarrassed. Heather continued to cry, first from the slap, but now she was crying from disgust with herself. *What am I doing? Of course, Aunt Neen is right. Jack is my son, not hers.* Through her tears, Heather said, "I didn't mean that. I don't even remember my mother. I'm just so scared to have him here. What if I can't do it? What if I fail? I am barely keeping everything together as it is."

Aunt Neen remained in her chair. She wanted to give Heather a chance to think this through for herself. Neen needed her to do this.

Heather took a deep breath, "Before you offered to come up on the weekends. Would you still be willing to do that?"

"I would love to. Every single weekend."

"Okay. Can I call you whenever?"

"Anytime. Day or night."

Heather was quiet. Neen needed her to believe in herself. "You can do this, Ina. Neen's Lakota dialect was heavy with emotion. "Our Creator has given you everything you need to raise up a wonderful Lakota wicha[6]. The Wakan Tanka[7] is asking you to be brave and strong."

"Do you care if Jack and I come this weekend so we can go trick-or-treating together?"

Neen didn't want to get her hopes up, but she couldn't wait to show Heather the outfit she had gotten Jack for Halloween.

"I think that would be a great idea."

---

6 Man

7 The Divine or Great Spirit

To Aunt Neen's delight, Heather did bring Jack home the following weekend. Aunt Neen couldn't help but notice how relaxed Heather was with Jack. Even after just one week, Neen could see the bond they were forming. Since Jack left, the house was so quiet. Neen welcomed the chaos of these two.

Halloween consisted of dressing Jack up in his first Pow Wow outfit and taking all sorts of pictures. They took him to a few houses, friends of Aunt Neen's, but then they were content to stay at home, playing cards and passing out candy for the rest of the night.

"Wow, if you had asked me two weeks ago what I was doing for Halloween, I would not have said this." Heather laughed, "But I am glad I'm here. And I love the outfit you got for Jack. Thank you, Auntie."

"You are welcome."

That Sunday Heather and Jack stayed as long as they could before having to leave. Heather hated driving at night, especially in the freezing temperatures.

Every Friday, Heather would get back from class to find Aunt Neen cleaning her apartment or rearranging furniture to make room for the new things she had brought with her. Heather had an apartment, but Aunt Neen was making it their home. Jack would be sitting in his swing or lying on the floor content watching the ceiling fan. Even then, he was the happiest baby.

By the middle of November, Jack was settled in with Heather. She was working hard on getting down a routine. He loved his day-care and, because it was right on campus, Heather could go see him between classes. November flew by with semester finals and keeping up with a very active seven-month-old.

Just as promised, Aunt Neen continued to travel from Mission every weekend to see them. Heather knew it was Aunt Neen's way of keeping Heather busy. And boy, did she. They toured the Prehistoric Indian Village, Corn Palace, and of course, the Carnegie Resource Center. Aunt Neen would request to take them to lunch at least one day while she was there. Each weekend consisted of a trip to the grocery store replenishing food, formula, diapers, and whatever else Heather needed to get through the week. Heather didn't have class on the Friday of Thanksgiving, so they made plans to spend the long weekend back home in Mission.

As the trip approached, Heather felt a growing sense of anticipation. They were heading into her favorite time of year, and now she had a son to share it with.

For Thanksgiving, Heather and Neen sat down and wrote out a menu. They both agreed, because Jack was now in the picture, it was time to bring back some of the old traditions which included a feast at Thanksgiving. Turkey, corn, wild rice, and pumpkin pie would be on the menu.

Christmas included going to the community center to make ornaments and decorate sugar cookies. The women and children loved playing with Jack, and they took turns holding him. At home, Neen and Heather filled Jack's stocking with baby books and toys. On Christmas Day, they dressed up in their bright colored dresses and attended Jack's first Christmas Day Pow Wow. Because Heather needed to get back to school, her and Jack were able to stay on the reservation just long enough to help Aunt Neen ring in the new year.

The first several months of 2018 were busy with classes and just being a young mom doing mom things.

Heather had lost touch with Lola. They tried for a while to keep up with their friendship, however Lola wanted Heather to always come over to her place. She always invited Jack as well, which was sweet, but Lola's idea of hanging out meant calling some guys and having some beers.

The one night they did go, Heather and Jack had left early, someone called Lola's apartment in for a noise complaint. She was busted for underage drinking. Heather was ready to put that friendship aside when Lola called Heather, completely bombed, accusing her of being the one that had called the cops.

Heather tried to explain it wasn't her, that she would have no reason to call the cops but Lola was talking over the top of her. Heather knew the conversation was going nowhere. The last thing she heard before she hung up on Lola was, "You better watch your back, Apple."

Chapter 6

April 2018

For Jack's first birthday, in April, Aunt Neen took them out to McDonald's and surprised Heather by inviting some of her classmates and their kids back to the apartment so they could do a smash cake for Jack. And although Heather's classmates were other young moms she had met through daycare and class schedules, Heather still missed Lola. She thought for sure if there would be a reason for Lola to reach out, it would be for Jack's first birthday.

In June they celebrated Heather's 21st birthday. Neen surprised her with a day of getting her hair and nails done. Instead of going out for drinks, they went out for ice cream.

Heather completed her first year of school with a 3.5 GPA. She signed up for summer classes and started working part-time at the hospital, which she loved. She was able to arrange her classes so that she was able to work and still pick up Jack by five. There was a church they attended right on campus. She and Jack were making Mitchell their home. She had been on a couple of dates, but nothing serious.

She and Jack had been to a July 4th party with friends. She was proud of herself for, once again, not having anything to drink.

Later that afternoon, when Heather and Jack were dropped off to their apartment, sun kissed and smelling like suntan lotion, Heather saw something laying in her yard under the front window. It was a brick. It had the word, "horror" written on it in black marker. She put it back where she found it, scooped up Jack, and quickly unlocked the front door and went inside. She locked the door behind her. As she grabbed some snacks for Jack from the diaper bag, she called Aunt Neen. She tried keeping her composure, she didn't want to frighten Jack, but the minute Aunt Neen picked up the phone, Heather started crying. "You need to call the police and report it. You need to have a record on file. You do that and I will call Elder Miller. I want there to be a record with tribal council as well. Call me back as soon as you get off the phone."

Heather did as Aunt Neen said and called the police department. They were going to send out a police officer. She called Aunt Neen back but Heather got her voice mail so she left a message.

As the police officer pulled up, Heather got a call from Aunt Neen, she hit ignore and instead sent a quick text message instead. "He's here. I will call you as soon as he leaves,"

"He took a picture of where it was laying and took it with him. He asked if I had cameras and since I don't, there really isn't anything he can do."

"Nothing at all? Did he ask you who you thought it could be?"

"He did, but I said no."

"Ok. Well, you tell me, then. Do you think it was Bobby?"

"How can it be? He's in jail."

In late July, Heather celebrated her official one-year sobriety. She was humbled by the fact that Aunt Neen and Elder Miller had driven to Mitchell to be there, however, the biggest surprise was when Lola walked in. The moment Heather saw her, she burst into tears.

"I'm sorry I was such an ass." Lola looked right at Heather, "Please forgive me."

"Of course, I forgive you! I am just so glad you're here! But honestly, it is just me and one other person receiving our medallion. You really didn't need to come."

"Are you kidding? I think this is the hardest thing a person can do. I am so proud of you!" Lola's voice dropped to a whisper. "In fact, do you care if I start coming to meetings with you?"

"I wouldn't mind at all. You can come anytime you want." Heather hadn't realized just how much she had been missing Lola, until she saw her walk in.

"I'm glad to see you two have finally made up." Aunt Neen brought over a glass of water for each of them. "What do you say, once this is done, we go pick up Jack from the sitter and go get some ice cream? After all, we need to celebrate!"

In August Heather was approached to do an internship for a new up and coming non-profit. She had met with her advisor and learned that this would be a paid position. Her advisor said she would be perfect for it. It was with an organization called "Walk America Clean". It was a non-profit that worked with communities across SD, including the reservations. They had two main goals within their organization; the first included helping people be clean from substance abuse, the second included keeping Mother Earth clean from trash. Both of these were accomplished just by walking. The message was clear – to be clean for generations to come, we must treat our bodies and Mother Earth the same; with reverence and respect.

The town of Valentine in Nebraska had recently implemented it. A young rancher started it in remembrance of his mom. The panel of speakers they had had on campus several months back had promoted the program. Since the South Dakota Governor was a big proponent of working with the reservations, he took this on as a new beacon of hope for South Dakota and its reservations. Heather was honored that her advisor thought of her to help get it going.

She liked the thought of joining an organization from the ground up. Heather was excited to learn more about it but she was worried she was taking on too much. However, her advisor did a great job of helping her see what she was capable of and reminding her that things worth having don't come easily. Following her meeting, Heather felt a new-found excitement. She could see her future and she was coming for it.

Heather's life was a full one; with Jack, school, work, church, her internship, and attending AA meetings, she was keeping busy. Aunt Neen slowly started to step back from helping. Now, instead of coming down every weekend, she was coming down once a month. Heather missed her Aunt Neen terribly; however, Lola stepped in when needed.

And although, Heather was experiencing horrible messages being sent to her through Facebook and to her email, she was determined to stay the course. She intentionally stayed busy to not allow herself to wallow in negative feelings. She remembered those emotions and how fast they could swallow one up. She had worked hard to find healthy ways to cope.

The life she was so scared of just a few months ago was a life she now craved to get back to at night. The smiles and hugs Jack would give her the moment she stepped in the room were her air. Most nights, Heather would read him a book, rock with him while she sang, and then lay him down in his crib. He would coo-coo for a little bit and then sleep. Every night she would whisper, "Mommy loves you so much." On the occasional nights when Jack was having a hard time falling asleep, or if Heather was exhausted, she would let him sleep with her. He would cuddle into her and she would breathe in his little baby scent. Heather knew his every mood, his every cry.

Yes, she had moments of anxiety, especially with the random messages that were still coming her way, but she would use what she learned at AA, she would allow herself to feel it, but not allow it to linger.

Jack continued to thrive at daycare. They would send her photos throughout the day of him playing in the park and trying new foods. He was a happy, chubby baby who was walking and exploring. They were building a beautiful life together, just her and her boy. Heather felt that the only missing link was a puppy. The apartment they lived in now did not allow pets but when Jack found a stuffed puppy at daycare, she immediately felt they needed a dog. He had complete meltdowns the first two days when he was told he had to leave the puppy behind. Finally, the daycare owner insisted they take it with them. From that point forward, Jack and his stuffed puppy were inseparable. Heather was certain the infatuation came from a puppy book he had been given for his birthday. And although the book was about several different puppies, Jack called all of them by the same name, Hawkeye. Heather liked the thought of having a pet. She liked the idea of having another companion around the house, an added sense of security. It was when Jack would remember Hawkeye in his nightly prayers, that Heather knew it was time to get serious about finding a furry member of the family.

In the middle of October, Heather moved into a small two-bedroom house, close to campus. A house that allowed pets.

Neen came down later in the week to help her organize her new house.

Heather discussed the matter of looking for a puppy, "Something not so big, but not too small, either."

Like a good Auntie, Aunt Neen went through all the reasons why getting a dog wasn't a good idea, however, Heather had given it a lot of thought and wouldn't be deterred. She assured her Auntie she would wait until spring as that would be the perfect time with the weather turning nice.

They agreed, between the two of them, they would make it work. Aunt Neen began to develop a plan. She knew a puppy would be a perfect birthday gift for Jack.

Heather started going through a box that consisted of everything from DVDs, to books to various knick-knacks for the living room.

"Auntie, I don't want to move again for a while. I know it is in our blood to journey, but I am determined to stay in one place for a while. I hate the packing, unpacking, blah, blah, blah. Also, I want Jack to know stability." Heather looked towards Jack, where he lay sleeping in his newly decorated room. The first room Heather put together was always Jack's. It was important that he felt like his room was his space, even as a baby, Heather thought it was important. While Heather was lost in different book titles, she didn't notice Aunt Neen grabbing a letter from her purse.

"Ina, I have something. It came to the house." She sat down beside Heather. "Have you heard from Bobby lately?"

Heather looked at the envelope Aunt Neen was holding in front of her. "I haven't, other than the occasional blocked calls that come to my phone. And I told you about the cryptic messages I'm sure came from him? He did leave a couple of messages a while ago, saying he thought he would be getting out soon." Heather didn't think much of the messages, with him receiving a seven-year sentence for selling drugs shortly after Jack was born, there was no way he would be getting out anytime soon.

"But, nothing lately." She turned the letter over slowly. It was from the SD State Penitentiary.

Heather's heart was pounding in her chest. Her life looked different now and she fiercely wanted to protect it. Somehow, she felt this letter was pandora's box.

She opened the letter, hands shaking. The writing was in blue ink and was on a yellow legal pad piece of paper. The writing was familiar, comforting. She read it quietly to herself and then handed it to Neen.

Dear Heather,

I really hope you decide to open this. I read my horoscope awhile back and it said try not to identify so strongly with your mistakes, just because you mess up sometimes doesn't make you a bad person, forgive yourself. That is what I am going by since I pray every day that my life will change for the better from here on

out. I know what I have to do, and I am going to do it. I am very confident in myself. I will prove it to everyone I can and I will change! I am going to do it. Anyway, I only have a few months left. Please give Jack a big hug for me and tell your Auntie I am sorry. I _am_ sorry, but, as you can tell, it hurt me too.
Love you, baby
Bobby

When Neen had finished reading the letter, she handed it back to Heather. She remained quiet.

"Well?" Heather sat on the floor in the living room of her new place, surrounded by the last few boxes left to go through from the latest move. She looked to Aunt Neen as her mirror.

"Well, I don't believe him. Actions speak louder than words. You have worked very hard for what you have. He must prove it to you with action."

"Yes. I agree." Heather's mind was reeling. *Doesn't it sound like he has changed?*

"You need to call the daycare immediately and let them know, no one is to pick up Jack and I mean *no one* except for you or I. Promise me, you will do that." Heather had not heard her Aunt Neen sound like this before. Almost irrational. "You know our Lakota men. They are full of pride and they are strong when they want to be. Sometimes that pride and strength can be misguided. Please, Ina, promise me, you will be careful."

"I promise, Auntie."

From that day on, Heather received a letter once a week. Then the phone calls started. Somehow, he knew her new phone number and knew where she lived.

It began with that one phone call. It had come from the jail early in the morning on a cool November morning. She was still lying in bed listening to her radio. "Better Man" had just come on. She thought, *How completely ironic.* She knew she shouldn't accept the call, but she did. After all, she was curious as to how he was doing.

If only she could go back and do it all over again... would she answer?

She couldn't go back now. Bobby had called her. Why she answered this time, when every other time she let it go to voicemail, she would ask herself for years to come.

Before she could say a word, he was asking if she had received his letters, and he was apologizing and begging her for forgiveness. He spoke to her in Lakota, which he knew she loved. Bobby was promising her he would get a good job or maybe he would go to college. He wants to be a good dad, the best dad for Jack.

He asked her about Jack. How much did he weigh now? What were his favorite shows? Heather missed talking to him. She answered all of his questions describing how Jack was in love with his stuffed puppy, Hawkeye. Bobby made reference to Jack never getting a rez dog but Heather didn't hear him clearly and decided to let it go. As she was talking to Bobby, she walked into Jack's room and saw him sleeping soundly.

Bobby was reiterating everything he had written in the numerous letters Heather had received. Heather could hear Aunt Neen's voice in her head, *Don't let him get to you. Don't believe him. He must prove it.* Heather pushed that voice away and instead allowed herself for just a minute to imagine a life with Bobby.

She sat down on the bed. Bobby was adamant in what he was saying, *"This life would be the exact opposite of how it was when we were dating."* They would both be clean and together, would go to school, raise their sweet boy, and be the happiest little family.

Heather listened to Bobby describe the life he saw for them. He sounded healthy and strong. *I have prayed for this day.* Bobby said he had met with the parole board and if he could prove he had a place to go and a support system, he could be out sometime in the coming months. He assured her he had passed all of the 11 RDT's[8] he had been given.

He said that life was his old life. He was ready to make his own way, and he wanted her and Jack to be a part of it. Right before he told her he loved her, he asked if, by chance, Heather could put some money in his account. Although her gut feeling was to tell him no, she could see he was really trying. She agreed she would as soon as they got off the phone. He told her he loved her and would call soon. Heather hung up the phone and went to find her debit card.

---

8 Random Drug Tests

CHAPTER 7

APRIL 2019

M am! Mam!" Jack was starting to find his words and mam was his way of saying mom. Heather heard the muffled cry coming from his bedroom. *Finally! He was awake!* They couldn't wait to start celebrating his birthday! Aunt Neen met Heather's eyes across the table. She was thinking the same thing. *Our boy is awake!*

Heather set her hot tea on the table and quickly went to get Jack. Aunt Neen followed Heather into the room, holding a chocolate cupcake. The bed covers were crumpled into a ball. Heather knew exactly where to find him. She started tickling the covers and soon heard his sweet giggle. "Happy Birthday, Baby!" Heather was so happy she could cry; she was filled with gratitude. Today, they were celebrating Jack's 2nd birthday, just the three of them.

Heather had finished her second year of school two weeks prior. And although she planned on staying in Mitchell for the summer, they came back home to celebrate Jack's birthday with Aunt Neen.

"Hey Buddy, look what Nana has! Should we go have a cupcake?" Jack was on his way to sit on Heather's lap until he saw the sweet treat. He scrambled from Heather's arms and held onto the quilt as he slid to the floor.

"Happy Birthday to you!" Neen started singing and Heather joined in.

Jack kept looking behind him to make sure they were still following. He pointed to his highchair and said, "Up!"

Picking up Jack, Heather gave him a quick hug before putting him in his high chair. Aunt Neen set the cupcake down in front of Jack and immediately the cupcake was squeezed into his hands and soon chocolate covered his face. "Silly boy." Heather laughed as she grabbed Jack's milk from the fridge. *Allowing Jack to have a cupcake first thing in the morning on his birthday; this will be a tradition of ours for years to come. One of many.*

Aunt Neen had made a quick exit from the kitchen and now was walking back in. She was holding something in her arms. What happened next was made for the movies. The sweetest, brightest moment, with sunlight streaming in from the east window. Their eyes met; a two-year-old little boy and his new, furry best-friend. Heather pleaded with God, *Please let me never forget this moment.* The blue heeler was the cutest puppy Heather had ever seen. Jack squealed and reached for the puppy.

Heather quickly wiped her hands and pulled Jack from his highchair, wiping the chocolate off his face. Her and Neen sat with him on the floor. The puppy immediately started licking Jack's face. Heather and Neen were laughing and watching every facial expression Jack made. Their family of three just became a family of four.

Once they were able to assure Jack that later that afternoon Hawkeye would be able to take a nap with him, Heather used the opportunity to run to the Dollar Store to pick up decorations and the grocery store to pick up a lemon cake for that evening. She was excited for this birthday, and they were going to celebrate again that night. Heather smiled thinking of her son.

Jet black hair like his momma and the prettiest green eyes. Those green eyes were one thing Heather could thank Bobby for. However, everything else about Jack was all Heather. He was determined to try things on his own, he laughed easily, he needed a light on when he slept. Jack was a fan of Elmo and Spiderman. His favorite food was pizza. He loved snuggles from his mom and Aunt Neen, who he called Nana.

It was coming up to the end of the month and Heather still had money in her wallet. She felt a rebirth of her dreams and goals.

Because of her job, she was able to save a little for his gifts and to make this day special for her little boy's second birthday. As Aunt Neen liked to say in a big boisterous voice, "Today is Jack's Day to lead the Big Parade!" Every time she said it Heather and Jack would giggle. What Heather didn't realize was Aunt Neen had a Children's book done for him that he would receive later that day, titled, *The Big Parade*, personalized with their names as the characters.[9]

Heather had just pulled up to the house. She dropped the visor down to take a quick peek at herself in the mirror. Most days she wore her hair up in a tight bun, but today she had it curled and pulled into a high pony. She took extra time to do her makeup, accenting her dark brown eyes with black mascara and highlighting her high cheek bones. The trail running she had started was evident physically and mentally. During her runs, she used those precious moments to talk positivity into her life. Reminding herself that she was worth hard work and that she deserved these hours to herself. She used running as her outlet, she also used it to find the warrior inside of her. She looked and felt like her old self. She didn't remember being this happy in a long time. She was so grateful for her sobriety.

She lifted up the visor. Aunt Neen was outside with Jack. She smiled. They had given Jack a small 4-wheeler for his birthday earlier that day and he hadn't gotten off of it since. Aunt Neen walked over to the car just as Heather was pulling up. Heather opened her car door.

"Do you need help with anything?"

Heather replied, "Yes, can you grab the cake out of the back?"

"Oh my goodness! He is going to love this Elmo cake!" While Aunt Neen grabbed the cake from the backseat, Heather reached behind her and pulled out all the bags full of party decorations and gifts.

As Heather and Aunt Neen were preparing to take the purchases

---

9   "The Big Parade" is a children's book by Karen M. Hefty

inside, a brown Chevy Impala pulled up. Before Heather had time to think, she dropped the bags and went to grab Jack. While trying to appear calm, Heather said, "Auntie, let's get inside." Heather had just enough time to grab a kicking and screaming Jack from the 4-wheeler, mad because he wanted to ride it, but Heather didn't care. She moved swiftly, carrying him to the house. Heather set Jack inside the house and held the door for Aunt Neen. Heather quickly reached down for Hawkeye and carried him into the house. Before she could get the screen door closed, a chill ran up her back.

As Bobby stepped out of the vehicle, he had a cigarette in one hand and a bouquet of blue carnations with a balloon that said, "Happy Birthday!" in the other. He took a long drag on his cigarette, threw it to the ground and yelled.

"Hey fam! – Daddy's home!"

Chapter 8

May 2019

t was Memorial Day weekend. Heather and Jack came back for the long weekend before her summer classes started the next week. Heather couldn't remember the last time she had been this nervous. She was wearing black leggings and a gray oversized hoodie. Her hair was in a low pony, and she had on a black cap. Her hoops were gold, and they matched the shades she was wearing. She had to admit, she felt like a badass in this outfit. She had gone for a slow jog when her phone rang. Bobby wanted to meet her. She was surprised when he agreed to go for a walk. The last time they had gone for a walk, just the two of them, was when they were in middle school. When the only thing they had to worry about was homework and getting home before dark.

Back then they loved exploring the land and following the train tracks. They would disappear in the morning and return before nightfall. They would go swimming in the creek that was hidden between the green lush hills of the reservation. They pretended to be their ancestors and would go searching for buffalo, deer, and coyotes. Most times they would only spot bunnies, bull frogs, and wild rhubarb. They would stop so the only thing they could hear was the wheat grass blowing in the wind.

Even at such a young age, those moments were meant just for them. They knew the beauty and message these creatures brought with them. It made them forge a bond between themselves and this land they were lucky enough to call home. During those summers Heather was never frightened. She only remembered seeing the beauty of the reservation. She loved listening to Bobby's grandfather talk about different herbs and recipes to aid in the ailments found among the people. His grandfather was a medicine man.

He was full of stories and told those stories to anyone who would listen. Bobby would play the part of interpreter because Grandfather told most of his stories in Lakota. On occasion, Bobby would get a word wrong, like when Grandpa was telling the story of the Great Grizzly bear rearing up and showing his bear paws; Bobby instead said the horse reared up and showed his horse paws. Grandfather would try not to laugh but soon the whole group would be laughing.

Bobby spent most of his time at Heather's, but when they would venture to his grandfather's, they only stayed while there was plenty of light in the day and would leave shortly after Bobby's uncles would arrive. Heather never understood why they always had to go so early. Only when she was older did she realize Bobby was protecting her. He was shielding her from the awfulness that had seeped into the reservation.

Back when they were younger, Bobby had the ability to include Heather as one of the guys but, when the occasion warranted, was also the first one to treat her like a lady. Heather remembered finding a book her Aunt Neen was reading, called *Gone with the Wind.* She wanted to dress up like Scarlett in the book, so she found some old table runners her aunt used at Christmas, and she glued them together to be a gold, glittery dress. She had taken gold garland and made a head piece out of it. That day Bobby decided to stop over. He laughed and laughed at her. And although Heather was mortified, Bobby didn't tell her nor would he ever just how beautiful she looked covered in garland and table runners with glitter all over her face.

It was in their 8th grade year, just after Bobby's 14th birthday, when the horrors of the reservation started to grab hold. His grandfather passed away earlier that year, and everything changed. He was lost and he was angry.

He didn't want to be around his family and when he was, he started to drink and smoke with them. Although he wouldn't talk to Heather about it, she knew they were hurting him somehow. He thought it was really cool when they let him drink with them and he didn't have to attend school if he didn't want to. When Heather tried to talk to him, he would become angry and would tell her if she didn't like it, she didn't need to come around. Somehow, that made her want to come around even more.

Aunt Neen started limiting the time Heather could be with Bobby. Now, looking back, Heather realized that was when she started to rebel. She started sneaking out, taking money from her aunt's purse, and lying to anyone she had to, to stay out of trouble.

Here she was now, so many years later, waiting for the boy who once was her warrior and protector. Now, a man, broken, trying to heal.

That healing part was the reason Heather asked if they could meet here at the City Park. The park was public and well-maintained and they never would have met here prior to him going to prison. Before, they would have met at the abandoned house or at a party. When she called Bobby letting him know she was home for the week, he said he wanted to meet. She was testing him. She wanted to do things differently this time. When she asked him to meet her at the park to go for a walk, she expected him to make up some excuse as to why it wouldn't work. Instead, surprising her, he said he would do anything she wanted, he just wanted to see her.

The sun was held in perfect balance with a light, cool breeze. Heather walked across the road and sat on the bench. Each sway from the nearby lilac tree pushed a calming scent towards her. While she waited, she sent a quick message to Aunt Neen, "How's Jack doing?"

"Totally fine. I just laid him down for a nap and I am relaxing with a good book. Take your time."

"Thank you, Auntie. Love you."

Auntie 'loved' the message with a heart emoji.

Heather smiled and leaned back to feel the sun on her face. When she looked up, she saw Bobby's Impala coming towards her. Again, she had the same feeling she had when he pulled up to Auntie's house on Jack's birthday.

She thought back to when she was little, before her parents died, she remembered times when unfamiliar cars would come to the house, the parents would tell the kids, "Go to the spot." The kids would hide under the floorboards or in the closets. Many times, it was the government coming to take them into custody. That Impala, when it first pulled up to Aunt Neen's, elicited those same feelings.

But it wasn't the government this time, it was just Bobby.

And although Heather agreed to meet with Bobby today and she wanted to believe prison was good for him, she also knew drugs were found in prison just as easily as on the reservation. She refused to allow Bobby to just assume he had a place with them. At first, Heather was irritated that he chose Jack's birthday as the day to come home. The party was supposed to be for Jack and his special day, not the fact that Bobby was home.

However, after the initial awkwardness and facilitating the introduction between Jack and Bobby, the day ended up being bittersweet. Jack's 2nd birthday celebrated with his mom, dad, nana, and new puppy.

Now, Heather's stomach was full of butterflies. *After everything he has done, why does he still have this effect on me?* Heather remained seated, thinking he would get out and join her, instead he rolled down his window, "Hey Babe, would you want to go for a drive with me?" Heather was not sure how to answer. She wasn't sure she wanted to get into a vehicle with him yet. Seeing the confusion on her face, Bobby explained, "Ok, before you answer, I was thinking we could go walk down by Grandfather's Lake. We could drive to the Five Oaks pasture and walk from there."

Heather could tell by the way he was framing his words that he wasn't high. And it appeared he had put some thought into this. "Yes. That sounds nice." Heather walked to the passenger side and jumped in. "Would it be ok if we walk to your grandfather's grave? I haven't been there since being back."

"Of course. I haven't been there since the funeral, so I would love that."

Heather was with the man she had loved for over half of her life. They had been through so much. Without taking his eyes off the road, Bobby reached for her hand, she laid it in his palm. It was the most natural thing to do. He wrapped his hand around hers. A tremor went through her. She wanted to make love. She wasn't sure if it was the familiar smell of his car or the tenderness he was showing, but she knew this afternoon would end with them making love. She sunk back into the seat and closed her eyes anticipating the afternoon ahead, settling in to this familiar feeling.

The ten-minute drive was filled with country music and small talk. Once they arrived at Five Oaks pasture, Bobby came around to Heather's side of the truck. He handed her a bottle of water, reached for her hand, and they easily fell into step with each other.

"Thanks for the water."

Bobby didn't respond. He was walking and looking up ahead.

Bobby had on Nike sweats and a long sleeve t-shirt. Heather was happy to see he had actually dressed for the occasion.

"I forget how beautiful it is out here." He squeezed Heather's hand. It was her turn to remain quiet. They walked for a while, not saying a word. She wondered what he was thinking. Her heart was pounding, and her mind was racing.

"How is my boy doing this morning?" It was a normal question, so why did she hate the way it was worded?

"*Our* boy is doing wonderfully."

"I want him to come stay a night or two with me." Heather dropped her hand from Bobby's. *So, this is why he wanted to meet with me today.*

"I think it's too soon. He doesn't know you, yet. I don't want him staying at the old house. Besides, we're leaving soon to go back home, to Mitchell."

"This is your thipi,[10] Chante' skuye'."[11] The words were whispered. Heather didn't respond. She wasn't ready to talk about Jack or their life in Mitchell or where she considered her home to be.

The last thing Heather wanted to do was ruin this perfect day because of her own insecurities. Instead, she changed the subject, "Do you remember how you would interpret grandfather's stories?"

Bobby stopped and looked at Heather. "Wow! It's been a long time since I've thought of that." Bobby laughed, "Was it as funny as I remember?"

"Yes... I wish we could go back to those times. We were so young and naïve."

Where they were walking it looked exactly how it did when they were exploring so many years ago. The only difference was the trees had grown even more into massive Ponderosa Pines.

They walked to the edge of the ravine; from there they could look down and see the lake nestled in with the pines surrounding the east and south side. The bright blue sky was competing with the horizon filling up the entire landscape. It was magical. Nothing could touch them here. Heather could hear their shrieks of laughter from a decade ago whispering through the wind.

Bobby looked at Heather, "What do you think? Should we walk to the lake before going to seeing grandfather?" Heather knew they were adding another hour to the day, but she hadn't seen Bobby like this in a long time, if ever.

"I would love that."

They arrived at the lake sweaty and tired. Before she could stop him, Bobby was stripping down and jumping into the water. Heather left her underwear and sports bra on, and jumped in shortly after. No one would be looking for them here. They were totally alone and secluded.

As for Heather, she felt like her world had just gotten 15 shades

---

10 Home

11 Sweetheart

brighter and a whole lot smaller. Her world, at this moment, was just herself and this boy, now man. The father of her child. The love of her life. Every nerve in her body was on fire. And the water rushing up on her intensified it.

She swam to Bobby, who was standing at the shallow end. She pulled her sports bra over her head and threw it on shore. She released her hair from the ponytail holder and let her hair tumble down over her shoulders. He wrapped her in a hug. He began to trail kisses from her ear, pausing only slightly at her neck before moving to her breast.

Chapter 9

June 2019

Since Bobby had gotten out of prison in April, he had wanted to move to Mitchell with Heather. Instead, Neen offered to rent an apartment on the reservation in the middle of town for Bobby, under the condition that Heather and Jack would stay in Mitchell until Heather finished her classes for the summer.

Bobby had no family in any position to help him, most of them also had been in trouble with the law so he couldn't list any of them as his respite. Yes, Neen wanted to help, but more than that, she didn't want him rushing into anything with Heather. Bobby declined Neen's offer, saying he was going to stay with friends.

Everything started out fine.

Bobby had secured a job with a construction company in Winner. His car had broken down, so he was catching rides with co-workers. He had been clean in prison, or so he said. He had told Heather he was reading a lot and the prison let him listen to self-help podcasts. Bobby had also received counseling, attending every week. Heather knew counseling was a big step for him and was shocked that he did it. According to Bobby, because he was a model prisoner, he was able to get out early. Really early. Neen was concerned it was too soon for him. She knew how addicted to drugs and alcohol he was on the reservation prior to going into prison. Aunt Neen had heard Bobby was wrapped up in a lot of illegal activities. She still had the feeling Bobby belonged in prison.

As Heather and Bobby started talking again, Aunt Neen begged Heather to be careful. Aunt Neen had seen this happen over and over. Although she gave nothing away, Neen didn't believe for one second that Bobby had changed.

Once again, he asked Heather if he could move to Mitchell with her. He had some good leads on some local construction jobs. He would help with rent, with Jack, and they could really start their life together.

She said it was too soon. She needed to take it slow, for Jack's sake. Jack didn't know Bobby. It would take time for that bond to grow. They compromised, Heather said he could visit her in Mitchell, but she refused to move back to the reservation. They tried it for a while in Mitchell. Bobby didn't have a job right away. He assured Heather he would help with grocery shopping and with Jack in between looking for employment. He didn't argue when Heather said alcohol would not be allowed in her house. He agreed they had both come too far to go back to that.

For the first week, it was exactly as Bobby promised. At 3:30 every day, he would walk to daycare to pick up Jack. When Heather arrived at home, Bobby would be making supper while Jack played in his room. Bobby loved it when her friends came over for pizza night. He told joke after joke. He loved being the center of attention. Bobby had invited Aunt Neen over for supper on several occasions, surprising Heather. Neen happened to be in town for doctors' appointments and she loved being able to see Jack while she was there. Heather knew her Aunt was trying to give them space and although Heather missed the days of just the three of them, this was the life Heather had prayed for so many times.

Her focus now needed to shift to making this family unit work. When the doubts crept in, she would think back to the love letters he had written to her from prison and the day they had gone on their walk. The long conversations talking about the life they both wanted. Why would he say all of that and go to all of this trouble if he didn't want it to work?

Eventually, she couldn't ignore what was happening. Daycare would call asking if anyone was picking up Jack that day. When

Heather would get home, she could smell alcohol on Bobby's breath. For a while he tried hiding it. It was around the same time Heather found out she was offered a raise and promotion at the hospital that she noticed she was missing money. He had taken $400 from Heather's rainy-day fund she had hidden in her tampon box, somewhere she thought he would never check. He showed up with a new Xbox and a bicycle for himself. When she asked where he got the money, he said he borrowed it from a friend. He outright lied to her. When she asked, she already knew he had taken it from her.

Bobby had told Heather he lined up a job in Winner. He would be starting on Monday. Heather had forgotten her phone so after dropping off Jack at daycare, she ran back to the apartment to grab it. It was already 9 am. Heather feigned surprise when she saw him, "I thought you were starting your job in Winner today?"

"They were supposed to call me and they haven't yet. Now you are checking up on me?"

Heather grabbed her phone off the coffee table. *Mmm, I thought I left it on the kitchen counter.* "No, I forgot my phone, I came home to grab it. I'm heading to work and I'm late." Heather was already thinking of the list of things she needed to get done that day.

"Give me your phone. You don't need it. You don't answer when I call anyway." Bobby was lying on the couch and although she didn't see any beer, she knew he was drunk or high. He came up on one elbow and said again very quietly, "Give me your phone."

"What for?" Heather took a step back.

Bobby jumped up from the couch and stumbled a little getting up. He put his face right up to hers and yelled, "Give me your phone!"

Heather was reeling. On the one hand, this was so typical of Bobby, but on the other hand she couldn't believe this was happening. Again. Bobby gave a small laugh and laid back down on the couch with her phone.

Heather knew there wasn't anything on there, but why did she feel guilty? She tried to speak calmly, "Why are you doing this? Thank God Jack is already at daycare. I won't let you talk to me like this in front of him."

"What are you hiding from me? Why do you want me to go back to the rez so bad? Oh, and just so you know, Jack is my kid too. And I will talk to his mother any way I want."

Now it was Heather's time to laugh, "Oh, ok! Mister tough guy. Seriously, you're not back for more than two months and you're already high or drunk even after you promised you wouldn't! It's 9 o'clock in the morning! What are you doing?" Bobby continued to look at her phone. Heather knew she should just walk away, but she needed some type of reaction to what she was saying. Didn't he see how much he was hurting her and their family?

"You are a liar and a thief. You didn't think I noticed you stole $400 from me? What man, what *dad* does that?"

Although Bobby continued to look at her phone, his head started twitching. She knew he was listening and he was about to explode. And yet, Heather couldn't stop talking, thinking about all of the empty lies she was told. All the promises he had made. *He has followed through with none of them.*

"Why did you even come here? You are miserable and you are making us miserable. I need someone I can depend on! Not a lazy, selfish wahtesni.[12]"

Bobby looked up and his eyes sent shivers down Heather's back.

Aunt Neen had tried calling Heather's cell phone several times only for it to go to voicemail right away. After the fourth time, Neen

---

12 Good–for–nothing one

called her at work. Heather's boss didn't have to say the words, she could hear the concern. "Heather didn't show up this morning, it's very unlike her. I tried calling her phone and it went straight to voicemail." By the time Neen had made the few preparations needed before leaving for Mitchell, it was already three. *Please don't let my girl be the next one that is missing. Please let Jackson be safe.* Aunt Neen tried to calm her thoughts but she also knew firsthand how these things could go. She had a feeling from the last time she was there, things were not good. Bobby, on a few occasions would joke about his friends that he could call on at any moment. They were the kind of friends who could 'take care of things.'

When Aunt Neen arrived in Mitchell, she went straight to Heather's apartment. She tried to calm her thoughts. She was thinking of the worst case scenario. As soon as she opened the door, she heard Heather talking to Jack. She let out her breath. She took a quick glance around the apartment and didn't see anything out of place. She ran around the wall into the kitchen.

Heather sat at the table, with Jack in his high-chair next to her. She looked up surprised, "Aunt Neen, what are you doing here? You just scared the crap out of me!"

Aunt Neen had to forget all of the things she was going to say, like, *"Thank God you are both here. Did you see I called? Why didn't you call me back? I was worried I would get here and you would both be gone. I know you didn't plan for it to go this way. I know you wanted to help Bobby find his own place. Of course, he didn't have a job right away and had no money and we know they wouldn't let him out unless he could give his parole agent an address he would be staying at. You wanted the family you have always dreamed about."* Instead, she said, "I couldn't get a hold of you and I missed you guys. I wanted to surprise you."

"Well, we are so glad you are here! I just got off the phone with my boss and she asked if I could come in tomorrow to make up some hours. Would you want to spend the night and watch Jackie for me?" Heather went to the refrigerator and refilled Jack's sippy cup. "Bobby is out of town for work for a couple of days." Neen could hear the inflection in Heather's voice. She was lying. Neen let it go for now, but consciously decided she would put that in her back pocket for later.

"I would love to!" Neen went to Jack and lifted him out of the high-chair and gave him a bear hug. "It is beautiful outside. Should we go to the park and then Walmart?" Although Neen wanted to ask Heather about why she wasn't at work when she called, she also knew Heather would eventually open up to her. For now, she was content to just be with them and to know they were safe.

Chapter 10

July 2019

After their awful fight, Bobby had left for a couple of days. When he got back, he told her he had gone to the rez to think some things through. He apologized and assured Heather that would never happen again. Who came and got him and brought him back was a mystery, but Heather didn't question him. She just wanted peace. He promised Heather he would attend AA meetings with her, but he said he needed to go back to his roots, to the place he called home. The construction company he had worked at before had a job waiting for him.

Heather didn't want to leave Mitchell. But she also wanted to know she tried everything she could to keep her family together. She was willing to take a month or so to see if her and Bobby could make this work. So it was decided: when she finished her summer class in June, they would go back to the reservation for the rest of the summer. Bobby said he had a buddy that was willing to let them stay at his place. It wasn't in the best shape, but Bobby promised he would do some work on it. His buddy was working out of state for the summer, so it worked perfectly.

Since Heather had enrolled for July classes, she needed to fill out the paperwork to withdraw. Her advisor was worried. She didn't want Heather to give up on her dreams. Heather was adamant she would be back for fall classes. In the meantime, Heather asked if it would be possible for her to implement the Walk America Clean campaign when she was back in Mission. Her advisor liked the idea. She said she would talk to the board and get back to her.

Heather called Jack's daycare and the hospital and told them about the situation and that she would be back by the end of August. She explained to them how she was going home to spend time with her family. Both said they would try to hold her spot but they couldn't guarantee it. Heather said she understood. *They know I'm coming back, right? But, for now, I need to focus on my family. We will worry about daycare and my job later.* After Heather hung up the phone, she sent Bobby a text. "Looking forward to this next month at home with you and Jack." She saw the 3 dots like he was going to text back, but nothing came through. *Must be busy packing.*

With help from her Aunt Neen, Heather kept her lease in Mitchell. It took them a couple of days to get packed. Of course, Bobby was in a great mood and on his best behavior. He talked about all the things they would do when they got back. He wanted to take Jack to the Pow Wow. "I want to do all of the things I missed while I was away, eat all the fry bread, do all the dances. We should host a big July 4th celebration. With the money I'll make at the construction job, we can fix up the house and look at trying to find you a newer vehicle. Maybe you can throw me a welcome back party." Bobby had such a way of ignoring the bad things going on around him, forgetting the past bad behaviors and expecting everyone around him to do the same. He certainly had a talent for making one believe that regardless of what had happened in the past, the future could be bright.

For the July 4th weekend, Bobby went out with friends, while Lola, Aunt Neen, and Heather spent the day with Jack. Aunt Neen had found a plastic kiddy pool at the Dollar Store along with Elmo arm floaties. Jack spent the whole day playing in the water and chasing Hawkeye in and out of the pool. Elder Miller had brought by sparklers and smoke bombs and Lola ended up bringing side walk chalk and bubbles.

Heather was excited when Lola had called Heather earlier in the week and asked what she thought about Lola bringing some of their friends down for the weekend. Heather said any other time, she would say yes, but because they had just moved back, she wanted to give Jack a little time to adjust. The truth was, Heather wasn't ready to share her life with their white friends. Those not from the reservation simply didn't understand their way of life. They would ask why they didn't have a TV, or why they didn't have any family pictures hung up. The things that white people took for granted, just weren't important on the reservation.

Lola seemed to understand and didn't push the situation. Now, they were sitting in lawn chairs out on the front yard. Elder Miller and Aunt Neen were inside preparing snacks and drinks. Heather and Lola had their chairs situated so they could see the community fireworks going off and still be able to watch Jack in his kiddy pool. It was right at dusk. The weather was perfect with it still warm but with a light breeze.

"Ok. So, tell me. How's it going here?" Lola had just opened a purple Shasta and sat down.

"Well, we haven't even been back for a full week, so I guess, ok?"

"And Bobby has started work?" Heather could feel her cheeks getting hot. Lola knew better than anyone how things were going.

"He hasn't, yet, but he is keeping busy working on his cars. I think he starts this next week. I don't want to be too hard on him. He's trying to get completely sober and-" Before Heather could finish her sentence, Lola broke in.

"Wait! That's what he's telling you? Where do you think he is right now? He is not sober, of that, I am certain!"

"What I was going to say is with sobriety, he can no longer hide from his feelings. So, we have been talking about him getting into some sort of counseling as well. I really do think he needs counseling more than anything. He does want to get better."

Seeing Aunt Neen and Elder Miller coming from the house, Heather wanted to change the subject. "Let's talk about something more fun. Instead of our friends coming here, should we plan a girls' weekend somewhere?"

"Yes, let's do!" Lola put her hand on Heather's arm. "No more negative talk from me, but please remember to take care of yourself and Jack. No matter what."

It wasn't long after they moved back that Bobby once again started showing the familiar signs of past behaviors.

"Bobby, it isn't a huge deal. I had budgeted for it, but Auntie wanted to help. I appreciated it."

Bobby was upset when he found out Aunt Neen had helped Heather buy Jack the 4-wheeler for his birthday earlier that year.

"Is that a dig at me because I wasn't here?"

"That is not at all what I meant."

"Well, I think he is too little to be riding it. It's too dangerous for him"

"He wears a helmet and there is a setting where he can only go so fast." Heather hated the way he made her feel like she had to explain this. As if she was incapable of raising their son. He should be thanking Auntie for everything she has done. *Who does he think handled all of this when he was in prison?*

"I think we should sell it. We could use the money to pay for rent or to pay Neen back. And, for that matter, we will get rid of the dog as well. I'm not wasting another penny on food for an ugly, stupid-as-fuck-rez dog. Don't be surprised if he turns up missing, most rez dogs do."

She had never seen Bobby hit or kick Hawkeye, but by the way Hawkeye cowered around Bobby she knew he had done something. Heather came home twice now to the door standing wide open and Hawkeye gone. Of course, Heather thought the worst the first time it happened. After a neighbor returned him and it happened again, Heather had had enough. One day before leaving for work she loaded up the dog and the 4-wheeler and took them both to Aunt Neen's. Once Bobby realized the 4-wheeler was gone he blamed her for selling it and keeping the money. She let him think whatever he wanted. And with Hawkeye, out of sight must have meant out of mind, because Bobby never once asked where the dog went.

At the end of July, Heather heard back from her advisor on giving her the go ahead to start creating awareness for the Walk America Clean campaign. She was able to set up a temporary office in the home of Elder Miller.

With his blessing, she began to share the history behind the home as well. Heather was able to research different grants and funding ideas both for the campaign and for the house. She remembered in Mitchell there were buildings on campus that had been added into the historical society. She was hoping to receive confirmation that Elder Miller's home also had been added. She just wasn't sure, since his house sat on reservation land. She filled out all of the paperwork and was hoping to hear back by the end of the week.

Heather tried to remain positive and focused on her future. Lola was also helping with the Walk America Clean campaign and was heading up the Mitchell office. Heather's favorite time of day was the 10 am standard morning meetings where they would get on a call and strategize different marketing ideas.

Those early days on the reservation filled Heather with optimism. Elder Miller had set up a small play area for Jack almost identical to the one Aunt Neen had set up in her office, so that Heather could bring him along when she was working. He had put a TV in there with a VCR player and had found a handful of Disney movies. Aunt Neen's office was within walking distance of Elder Miller's. Heather had to laugh during one of the phone calls with Lola, she asked how things were going and Heather said, "We're living as close to a Hallmark movie as you can get on the reservation."

Heather hardly saw Bobby at all during the day. When she asked him why he didn't come around more often, he said he didn't want to interrupt her at work. She knew that in reality he didn't come around because he didn't get out of bed until noon and he didn't want to see Elder Miller.

At night, the partying was getting out of hand. It would start as friends coming over to 'help' with this or that and eventually nothing would get done and everyone would be drinking and smoking pot, amongst other things. And there would be yet another broken down vehicle in their yard.

Bobby was starting to pressure Heather into staying up late. Heather was struggling with being a good mom and trying to keep the peace with Bobby. It was important for Jack to get to bed at a decent time and he and Heather had gotten into certain routines while they were in Mitchell. Heather laying down with him until he fell asleep was one of those, taking baths on specific nights was another. It was those routines that helped Heather with her sobriety.

When they first moved back to the reservation, Bobby didn't make a big deal about it. However, as time went on, he would make comments like, "I'm not raising a sissy boy" and "before we know it, we are going to have a 'tit baby.'" Heather hated it when he talked like that. There were several times when Bobby had friends over and Heather would be carrying Jack into the house or to bed and everyone would erupt in laughter. She assumed she and/or Jack were the butt of their jokes.

She was also worried about her own mental health. She could swear she would set her alarm clock and yet her alarm wouldn't go off, causing her to oversleep. She had gotten to work late a couple of times. The first time it happened; she told Elder Miller about it. After it happened several more times, she started making up excuses as to why she was late; never saying it had anything to do with Bobby. The only person who knew exactly what was going on was, Lola. "Change your password on your phone. Don't let him get away with this. He will sabotage everything you have worked for."

Bobby was becoming erratic, calling Heather several times throughout the day, so much so that she had to start putting her phone on silent. If she didn't answer, he started to randomly show up at her office. Elder Miller pulled her aside one day and asked if everything was ok at home. For a brief moment Heather thought about telling him everything. And yet, she worried she would say the wrong thing and her Auntie would find out. Aunt Neen had warned her this would happen and she didn't want to admit yet, just how right her Auntie was.

She could feel herself reverting back to the way she was before having Jack and, although she knew she didn't want to go back to that, she was forgetting how to cope. She had attended only one AA meeting since she had been back.

Bobby still wasn't working, but was getting money from somewhere. She felt herself becoming negative, paranoid, and angry. She was stuck again, trying to dream of a better future, knowing she needed to leave Bobby, but she felt she needed to stay at least until the end of August. Plus, she loved the work environment she had created for herself. She didn't want to leave the couple of projects she had started unfinished.

Her and Bobby were starting to fight all of the time and Jack was having meltdowns. On this particular day, Bobby was drinking again when she came home for lunch. She went back to work without incident. But she was scared to see what she would find when she got home that night. She decided to leave Jack with Aunt Neen.

As Heather pulled up to the house, two cars were leaving. She didn't recognize either one of them. When she walked in, the house had the familiar smell and green haze that told her they had been smoking pot. She was ready to have this out with him. She was ready to be done. "Bobby, we need to talk."

Bobby was at the fridge grabbing a beer. "Ok. Let's talk."

Heather sat down at the kitchen table. It was an old metal table and the chairs were random ones Bobby had picked up at a garage sale. "First of all, did you see the water and electric bill on the counter yesterday? Those need to be paid. It's your month. And secondly, I'm moving back to Mitchell. I need to get Jack out of here or he is going to end up like us. I was going to wait until school started, but I need to leave sooner."

Bobby sat down at the table across from her. He cracked open his beer and took a big guzzle, some of it dripping off his chin from drinking it too fast. He ignored the first question. "He isn't going to end up just like us, what you mean is, he will end up like me."

Heather moved her chair closer to the table. She pushed the overflowing ash tray towards Bobby. "Can I ask you something?" Heather didn't wait for him to answer, "How is this enough for you? When we were younger, we always said this wasn't the life we would have. Remember, you wanted to be a firefighter?"

Bobby laughed, he grabbed a cigarette from the pack that was sitting on the table, lit it and said, "I do remember. That was short-lived. Once I realized I needed to pay for training and stay sober." The smoke floated from his nostrils and seeped from his mouth. "Baby, look around." He took another long drag on his cigarette, blowing a smoke ring. "This is what we know. Our ancestors bled, fought, and died for this. It is our land now and our right to stay here. We need to come up with new dreams, right here."

Bobby paused, and took another big drink, "What's in Mitchell, anyway? Did you meet someone there? Maybe an apple picker?" Bobby laughed. Heather stood up, "Ok, I'm leaving. I'm not listening to this. I'm trying to have a decent conversation with you."

"Ok, Ok! Just sit down. But you know the only thing that's in Mitchell is people telling you what to do and how to do it. Here, we can come and go and do whatever the fuck we want, and no one says a word. Think about how hard it will be to take care of Jack all by yourself. The tribe won't protect you if something happens." As Bobby was talking, Heather was only half-listening, she had already made up her mind: She was moving back to Mitchell.

For the next several days, she walked on eggshells. Her thoughts were consumed with leaving. While at work, she called a few of her friends to fill them in on her plans. She asked them not to post anything on social media. She called her landlord and asked if he would make sure the utilities were turned back on as she would be heading back within the week.

At night, she slept with Jack. Before bed each night, she whispered her prayers to him. She would say them in English and then would say as much as she could in Lakota. Bobby didn't come in the house until they were in bed and most days her and Jack were gone before Bobby woke up. She was grateful because it seemed he had agreed to be amicable without saying it out loud.

The next day, Heather went home on her afternoon break. She remembered Bobby saying something about not being home before dark as he had 'errands' to run. Seeing his car in the driveway when she pulled up almost made her turn around. The last thing she wanted today was a confrontation. But, more than that, she wanted to take one little step towards her plan. She didn't want him to control her anymore.

Her plan was to slowly start taking things to Aunt Neen's. Things he would never notice were missing. The door was sitting wide open and there were empty beer cans everywhere. There was a visible haze over the living room and kitchen, it smelled like cigarettes, marijuana, and sweat.

She walked in and immediately saw that Bobby was sitting on the couch and had that wathogla[13] look in his eye. He slowly lifted his head towards her, and his beautiful green eyes had turned into huge black discs. He asked her in slurred words, "What're ya doin' here?"

"I'm on a late lunch break, I just stopped in to grab some things really quick." Heather answered as calmly as possible. "I didn't know you would be home. For some reason I thought you said you weren't going to be home before dark? Your plans must have changed?"

Bobby ignored her question and instead mimicked her and said in a high-pitched voice, "Your plans must've changed." He lit a cigarette and blew out a stream of smoke. "Where's yer son?"

She hated it when he brought up Jack. She felt it was his way of threatening her. She was petrified that if she told Bobby where Jack was, there was a good chance he would go get him.

---

13 Wild, scared

"He's with Aunt Neen. They're running errands."

Heather went to the cupboard in the kitchen to check for Advil. She had a massive headache. Of course, the bottle was empty.

"Grab me a beer." Heather's instinct was to tell him no, it was too early in the day, and she didn't want another repeat of last night and the night before that. But instead, she did what she was told. She needed to get back to work as soon as possible.

She went to the fridge and pulled out a Budweiser tallboy and took it over to him. "You have one left."

He mimicked her again in a high voice, "You have one left." He then went back to the slow, low voice that sent a shiver down her back. "Then get me more."

Heather said in a lower voice, "I don't have any money for beer." As she said it, she wished she could retract it.

He jumped up and grabbed her arm. "What did you do with the twenty bucks I gave you?" Heather wanted to laugh in his face. *Twenty bucks? Is he worried about twenty bucks?*

Heather turned her head so he couldn't see her face, "I used that for milk, mac and cheese, and ramen noodles for Jack. Thank you by the way... for helping." The words felt like poison on her tongue. She was so used to this behavior. Him trying to intimidate her, her trying to talk him down to whatever level of normal it was for that day. She was sick of it.

He smelled so bad; she was certain he hadn't showered in several days. His greasy, black hair was pulled back into a ponytail and he was wearing a dull gray bandana. She did a quick survey of her surroundings. Something seemed off. She saw a brown paper bag on the floor. *Is that a hand gun? What is happening? Was he going to kill himself? Or was he waiting for me?*

"Heather!" She was jolted back to reality by his awful voice that sounded more like an animal growl. He grabbed her face and yanked it towards him. She yelled out in pain, "Don't even think about doing something dumb. I can see that look in yer eyes, like you think you would have it better somewhere else." He whispered into her ear, "Yer not leaving me and yer not taking my boy. Do you understand?"

He let go of her face and took a swig of his beer. When he talked again, she could feel spit mixed with beer on her face. "Take off your clothes. Give me a blow job. Show me you love me. I need you to show me. Please, Heather." Her brain was spinning. *He isn't himself right now.*

She wanted to throw up. "You know I want to, baby, but I don't have time today. I will the minute I get home this afternoon."

He yanked the back of her head and pushed her to the ground. "I ain't asking, you mother fucking thaspah suka."[14] He was undoing the zipper on his pants. Back in the day, Heather would have panicked. Not anymore. She knew he wouldn't be able to get hard. She also knew she just needed to play nice a little bit longer and he would give up, not wanting to embarrass himself.

"Ok, ok, baby." She whispered. She went to her knees and grabbed his penis with her hand and started to rub it. She was disgusted. It was limp and even though she licked it with her tongue, it was not moving or changing in size. She smiled as she looked up, pretending as if she were trying to make him feel better. "Do you want me to try something else, baby?"

Normally, he would walk away, grab a cigarette and sit in the chair with his pants still down. But today was different.

Today was the day she would look back on for many, many years to come and know that this is what it took for her to finally leave. He remained very still. He grabbed his beer can and dumped the remainder over her head. He pushed her down onto her back and spread her legs, shoving the beer can between them.

Heather was petrified. "Please don't do this, Bobby. It hurts." For a brief moment she thought about grabbing for that brown paper sack. Something had overtaken him, and she was scared he wouldn't come out of it. She didn't dare try to get up. She realized he was

---

14 Apple bitch

getting off the more she made it seem as if she was enjoying it. She felt sick, she couldn't believe this was happening. She moaned and writhed and acted like she had orgasmed. Finally, he removed the can from inside her and laid on top of her. He grabbed her face and whispered to her, "I knew you would love that. Maybe tonight we can try some other things." He licked her all over her face.

She was desperately trying not to throw up. Her brain shut down, she was numb, not sure how she got here, how this could happen. She mentally removed herself from that place and began preparing herself for everything she needed to do to leave, for good. She was not going to bring Jack back here. He would stay with Aunt Neen. She would go to work and go directly to Aunt Neen's. Aunt Neen would keep her safe and would help her come up with a plan. Heather looked to Bobby. He had rolled over on the floor and was snoring loudly. She hurried to pull up her pants. She ran to the kitchen and double checked the faucet to see if, by chance, he paid the water bill. Nothing. She would have to clean herself up elsewhere.

Heather ended up going straight to Aunt Neen's house. She couldn't go to the office smelling like booze and sex and she was in no frame of mind to see anyone. When she got to the house, she saw the look of horror on Aunt Neen's face, "Oh my God, niecie, what happened?"

Heather started crying "I don't know. I – don't – know what's happened to me." She felt as if she was in someone else's body. She kept patting at her clothes and her hair. Was she raped? Did Bobby mean to hurt her? Heather couldn't catch her breath. She was crying so hard, she was hiccupping.

"Come on, come sit at the table or do you want to shower? Should we call the police? Do you want me to call Elder Miller? Niecie–did Bobby do this?" When Heather didn't say anything, Neen kept talking.

"Niecie, please tell me you are getting out of this situation! Please, you need to move back to Mitchell. I worry history is repeating itself. I am scared for Jack... and you. Remember, what we talked about so many times before, when you were pregnant? Jack needs a better life, a better start. You are strong and capable of showing him what a healthy life looks like. Thank God Jack is napping. He can't see you like this."

"Yes. I remember. And we're going to move back to Mitchell as soon as we can. But today – today, he showed me exactly what he can do. He had a gun there." Heather sat in Neen's chair. Neen grabbed the blanket from the couch and wrapped it around Heather's shoulders. Heather enveloped herself with the blanket "He knew I was supposed to be at work and he made me do awful things." Her voice caught in her throat, "I-I thought about grabbing the gun, Auntie. I thought about it." Heather rambled. "I *know* I need to leave but he will take Jack from me. He will kill me. If he knows how serious I am about leaving, he will kill me." Heather finally said the words out loud. She had thought them many times, but to vocalize the fact that she thought Bobby was capable of killing her; made her dizzy.

"Listen to me, Niecie. You may have to do the dance with him." Aunt Neen handed Heather a Kleenex. "Listen–you have to stop crying and listen to me - have you heard the phrase, float like a butterfly, sting like a bee?"

"I think so? Something to do with a boxer?"

"Yes, Muhammad Ali described his fighting style like that. That is how you need to look at this. You are in the boxing ring with him. Give him no indication as to what your next move is going to be... but, start developing a plan right now. And be ready to leave. You will know when the time is right. Trust your instincts and when you doubt yourself, remember to float like a butterfly and sting like a bee.

Heather did as Aunt Neen suggested. Heather made up with Bobby the following day. She became the loving, supportive girlfriend she knew he wanted her to be. So, when the escape night came a few weeks later, he didn't see it coming. The night started as any regular night. Bobby and his friends had several days of partying behind them, a few of them were outside helping with something on his truck. They were drinking beer, smoking cigarettes and weed, listening to Lynyrd Skynyrd. Soon they had moved inside. Heather had gone in to lay with Jack. As the music and voices got louder, she pulled Jack close to her.

She lay there wide-awake knowing she could not do this anymore. Once she heard the party die down and was certain Bobby and his friends had passed out, she laid there, listening for any little sound. She lay there feeling the warmth of Jack while debating with herself. *Doesn't Jack need both of his parents? I could just wait and not leave until the end of August like I had planned. Bobby will have no one if we go. But I can't have Bobby treating me the way he does, especially as Jack gets older. Jack deserves the best life... right now, this is not it.* Trying to muster up the courage to leave, she closed her eyes. *I heard it only takes three seconds of courage to change the entire trajectory of one's life. I need those three seconds right now.* She took a deep breath in and out. She closed her eyes and visualized where she set her clothes and shoes out the night before. She ran through exactly what she was going to do and how she was going to do it. *Float like a butterfly... sting like a bee.*

She opened her eyes. She again took a deep breath in and slowly let it out. She laid completely still while her eyes adjusted to the darkness. *Float like a butterfly.*

She rolled away from Jack and onto her stomach. She reached down to the floor and grabbed her phone, 3:13 am. She thought about turning on the flashlight and then thought better of it. Now that she had decided she was leaving, she moved swiftly and quietly in the dark of night. She pulled on the clothes she had set out earlier and grabbed the bag she had put together. She picked up Jack and hugged him to her. He whimpered and Heather held her breath. Her heart thumped as loud as the bass music that had been playing earlier.

What would Bobby do if he woke up seeing me leave in the middle of the night? And especially with Jack? The reality of the situation hit her hard. *He would murder me.* Her heart started thumping again in her chest. *Float like a butterfly.* She just needed to get out of the house and get to her car. *My car.* The one thing she hadn't thought about was her car. *What if someone parked behind me? What if my car for some fluke reason won't start?*

She calmed herself and reached into her pocket to grab her keys. Her fingers searched but she couldn't feel them. *Where are they? Oh my God! Where are my keys?* She heard a whisper, *Remember, you put them in the side pocket of the bag.* She shifted Jack to one arm and reached into the bag on her shoulder. Like a crown jewel, Heather's hand closed around the keys.

Something in Heather told her she needed to go. Now! Although, she wanted to run, she forced herself to be methodical in her actions. Heather turned towards the bedroom door and listened again for any type of movement. As she opened the door, she hugged Jack to her and allowed her eyes to adjust to the dark objects that were scattered on the floor and the couch. She could hear the deep breathing sounds of sleep. *Float like a butterfly.*

As she made her way through to the front door and onto to the step, the outside light came on. *Of course, it comes on! Nothing else in this house works but that light sure does!* Heather walked directly to her car. She threw the bag onto the passenger seat and, with Jack in her left arm, she sat down behind the wheel. She counted to herself: 3, 2, 1. She started the car and backed it out of the driveway. *Sting like a bee.*

⌇——╫——⌇

Once she pulled into Aunt Neen's, she let out a big sigh of relief. She didn't realize she had been holding her breath. They were greeted at the door by Hawkeye, as if he knew they were coming. He didn't bark but wagged his tail and followed them right into Jack's room.

Jack is safe here. She tucked Jack in. She remembered to go back out to lock the door. Soon after, she laid down with Jack, Hawkeye also jumped onto the bed. He was another form of her security blanket. Heather took a deep breath and thanked God she had decided to come here. She finally started to relax. Here, she didn't worry about someone trying to climb into bed with her, or someone turning the lights on looking for their drugs or bong. Here, she knew when they woke up, they would have running water, a hot shower, and a decent breakfast. This was their home.

Heather slept a couple of hours before work. When she woke, Jack and Hawkeye were still sound asleep beside her. She could hear Aunt Neen moving around in the kitchen. She slowly got out of bed. She gave Jack a quick peck on his forehead, "Love you, little boy." She whispered to him. Aunt Neen was finishing watering her plants when Heather walked out in the long shirt she had worn to bed.

"Did you do it? Finally?" Neen sat the water jug on the counter and grabbed a couple of tea bags and the tea kettle from the stove. Heather sat down at the table and, pulled her cup from the day before towards her. "Auntie – we need to call my landlord in Mitchell. Jack and I need to go. And please, please consider coming with us."

Chapter 11

August 2019

After leaving Bobby's that night, Heather and Aunt Neen, along with Jack and Hawkeye, met with Elder Miller the next day in his garden. Every time Heather visited the gardens, she was reminded of the first time she saw it. She still felt the same sense of awe and peace she felt that first morning when she was coming into recovery. Since Heather had been home throughout the summer, they had done some improvements adding a water fountain and a wrought iron patio table with chairs. The temperature was 87 degrees and rising. The babbling sound of the water fountain and the kaleidoscope of colors exploding all around them, made for a heaven on earth.

"I love it here." Heather said the words to herself. She put Jack on the ground for him to explore as she sat at the table. Noticing Elder Miller walking towards her with a pitcher and glasses, Heather jumped up. "Can I help?"

"No, no. I've got it." Heather had come to know Elder Miller and she knew there was no way he would accept her help, but she offered anyway.

They each sat at the table. Aunt Neen removed the leash from Hawkeye's collar to let him run a little. Elder Miller poured ice tea into the glasses. "Have you heard from Bobby?"

"No, but I am sure it's only a matter of time."

"I agree. At this point, it hasn't set in that you have left for good. You need to let me know if you have any issues with him. In the meantime, you are either at home or here. Jackson is with one of us at all times."

"Yes." Aunt Neen looked at Heather. "I think we can all agree you and Jackson need to get back to Mitchell as soon as possible."

"Auntie, I want you to consider moving back with us." Heather was looking for collaboration from Elder Miller. Elder Miller remained silent. "Perhaps down the road, we can look at that, Ina, but for now, my place is here. I have to finish my work with the MMIW and with you back in Mitchell, someone will need to help with the Walk America Clean campaign. You don't need to worry about me." Heather could tell by the look on Aunt Neen's face, it would do no good to argue with her. Her mind was made up.

"Ok, thinking ahead, I am wondering if you shouldn't look at moving to a different apartment. The word on the street is that Bobby has been making frequent trips out of town. I don't know what he is up to, but it is something." Elder Miller looked at Heather as if waiting for an answer.

"I have no idea. I mean, I know he is getting his weed and cocaine from somewhere and it wouldn't surprise me in the least if he is dealing."

Aunt Neen lowered her voice. "Ina, you were allowing Jackson to be around that?"

"Did I really have a choice?" Heather could feel the heat settle into her cheeks. Her Auntie had never said anything like that before. "And really, when Bobby is sober, he is the old Bobby, the Bobby before his grandpa died. It is only when he is drugging it up that he becomes a person I don't recognize. And that person is coming around more and more. That is why I had to leave; for Jackson but also for my mental health."

"And remember, wakhanheza,[15] you are now sober. You are look-ing at all of this from a different lens. If only we could get Bobby to let go of the past. When our Creator brought us here, he did

---

15 Child

not want us to live in sorrow and pain. I have to believe a new day is dawning. I suppose we must find our patience." Heather loved hearing Elder Miller reflect on the past and in his own way, reclaim the future. He and Auntie embodied the beautiful collision of past traumas with present day hope. Heather truly felt this moment was magical and generational. She could feel all of them connected to the generations of the past as well as those far into the future.

When it was time to leave, Elder Miller hugged her. As always, he whispered, "Peace, sister", but today he said it in Lakota. She carried those words like a prayer, letting them wrap around her, steadying her spirit and lighting the path ahead.

Heather started making the calls to get back to Mitchell. And although her landlord, earlier in the week, had made it sound like things would be ready by Sunday, he now said he needed to do some painting, so she would need to wait a couple of weeks before returning. Heather was confused as to what had changed, but she also appreciated him wanting to update the place.

In the week that followed, Heather kept busy by applying for more grants. She had also been in contact with the Governor from Nebraska. He had asked if she would be available to come in and talk about the Walk America Clean campaign. He was a friend of Carol's, Heather's Financial Aid officer and she had been talking very highly to him about all of the work Heather had been doing. Heather immediately called Lola and told her the good news. "When will you be back? We need to celebrate!" Even through the phone, Heather could hear Lola smiling.

"Hopefully, next week. I have so much to tell you, but I need to get Jack down for his nap. Let's catch up when I get there! I will see you soon!" As they went to hang up, Heather said, "Lola!" But it was too late, Lola had already clicked off. *Shoot! I should have asked her how the apartments were looking!*

One week had passed and she had just gotten her first text message from Bobby. "Hey, baby. I'm sorry. Why did you leave?" Heather ignored the text. She proceeded to receive ten more texts that day. Each one becoming a little more desperate. Aunt Neen encouraged Heather to block his number, but she couldn't do it. After everything he had done, and no matter how scared she was, she couldn't completely turn her back on him.

Her landlord called and said the apartment would be ready by the next Sunday. Heather let him know she would be there Sunday after lunch. She mentally started preparing a list of everything she needed to do before leaving.

Bobby tried calling. When she wouldn't answer, he would immediately send another text. He knew exactly what to say to get her attention. In a voice recording to her, he was pleading. Bobby said he was sorry about all of the partying and he had called Elder Miller that morning about being his sponsor. He was adamant that he was going to get into AA again. Still, she didn't respond. He left another recording saying he was accepted into in-patient therapy in Nebraska. He would be leaving that following Monday. He asked if Jack would want to come over and roast marshmallows before he left.

Heather had the day off from work and Aunt Neen wasn't feeling well, she was resting in her chair. Hawkeye was squeezed in beside her with his eyes peeking out from under the blanket that was draped over Aunt Neen's lap.

Heather sat down on the footstool in front of Aunt Neen. She read the text messages to Aunt Neen and played the voice recordings. Aunt Neen didn't say anything. "Well, what do you think? The fact that he first tried calling at 9 am, tells me he didn't party last night." They heard fussing from Jack. He had lost interest in his breakfast and so Heather moved him from his high chair down to the floor beside his toys.

"I think actions speak louder than words. I think he is manipulating you and he knows exactly what to say. Do you want me to call Elder Miller and ask him? He would tell me if Bobby called him. I can call over to the recovery center and confirm with them as well."

"No, I don't think he would lie about any of that. He knows we could call." Heather picked up Jack and bounced him on her lap. "He has no family. No healthy family, anyway. If we give up on him totally, then what will he have?"

"It sounds like your mind is made up. I just ask one thing. Do not tell him you are leaving. Let's get you back to Mitchell and then we can seriously talk about trying to help Bobby again."

Heather was talking to Aunt Neen, but she was saying the words out loud to quiet the doubts screaming in her head. "If we go over there, I will have my phone and we will leave the minute there's any trouble. I feel like it's the least we can do before we leave and especially for him, before going into treatment."

Heather grabbed her phone from her back pocket and sent a quick text to Bobby saying they would come over for a couple of hours.

"What can I get you before we leave?" Heather placed Jack on Aunt Neen's lap and he snuggled into her.

"Maybe some chicken noodle soup and hot milk?"

"Coming right up!" As Heather waited for the soup and milk to heat, she double checked Jack's bag.

"Thank you, Ina." Heather placed the soup and milk on Aunt Neen's TV tray. She lifted Jack from Neen's lap and set him on the floor. She pulled the foot stool to the side and then carefully pulled the TV tray over to Neen's chair.

"We're only going over there for a couple of hours. I have my phone! I love you." Heather gave her a quick peck on the cheek.

Aunt Neen waved her off, "Love you, too." She yelled, "Love you, Jack! Have fun with daddy!"

Jack yelled back as he was walking out the door, "Wuv you!" Heather appreciated Aunt Neen trying to be so positive when it came to the relationship between Jack and Bobby. Heather was aware of what Aunt Neen's true feelings were, but you would never know those feelings when she was talking to Jack.

Heather grabbed Jack's backpack that was sitting by the door. The bag was full of snacks, bottled water, and a variety of his toys. Heather was certain Bobby would have none of those things at his place.

Heather mentally prepared herself for what she was going to deal with once she got to Bobby's. She was certain the house would be a mess. Without her there, nothing got put away or cleaned up. Anything he ate would be left out on the counter, anything he wore would be left right where he took it off. She reminded herself to keep her mouth shut. She didn't live there anymore and how he lived was up to him. She looked into the rearview mirror and saw Jack looking at her. "Love you, buddy." Jack babbled something in return and then grabbed his sippy cup. Heather was at peace with the decision to go and yet scenes from the last time she was there kept playing in her mind.

As soon as Jack was out of the car Bobby picked him up and said, "How's daddy's little man?" Heather's guard was instantly up. Even with Bobby's comment, she felt as if he was telling her: *Jack is mine and you better not forget it.* Jack didn't fight being picked up, but he didn't snuggle into Bobby the way he did with her or Neen. There was one day when Bobby had picked up Jack and Jack said in an innocent two-and-a-half-year-old way, "You stink!" Heather had held her breath, wondering how Bobby would react. Bobby threw his head back in a big laugh and said, "Boy, this is the smell of your legacy, an Akicita!"[16]

Today, Bobby looked nice. He had dark blue jeans and a green and black plaid long sleeve shirt neatly tucked in with cowboy boots. It had been almost two weeks since she had last seen him. Had he lost weight?

They walked into the house and Heather was surprised to see

---

16 Warrior

it cleaner than she had seen in a long time. Bobby was in a great mood. He looked right at Heather and said, "I thought we would build a fire out back and roast some marshmallows with Jack."

Heather said right away, "Oh, I didn't bring stuff to make marshmallows."

"No need." Bobby said, pleasantly enough. "I have some friends coming over with their kids. They're bringing everything we'll need for a great day." Seeing the look on Heather's face, Bobby said, "Come on, don't look like that!"

The hair on Heather's neck stood up. *Already, nothing he told me is happening.* The voice in her head said to leave now. *I'm not doing this today. I am not going to read into every little thing. Today we are staying for a couple of hours and we're going with the flow.*

Bobby set Jack onto his feet and gabbed a cup from the cupboard and a gallon of milk from the fridge, whistling the whole time. Heather didn't remember the last time she had heard Bobby whistle. She loved this version of him. He handed the cup of milk to Jack but before Heather could stop him, Jack lifted the cup to his mouth, spilling it down the front of his shirt.

Again, Heather cringed, waiting for the impatient tantrum to expel from Bobby. Instead, Bobby walked to his room and came out with a stack of clothes and three sets of shoes, all for Jack. He also brought a pack of baby wipes. Seeing the look of confusion on Heathers' face he said, "My friend has a baby, and these were left here." Jack had been potty trained for several months; Heather knew they weren't from Jack. Bobby grabbed a couple of the wipes from the container and wiped the milk from Jack's shirt. *Who is the guy?* Heather thought to herself.

"Pick out a new outfit, Jack. What do you want to wear?"

Jack didn't move. "Come on, buddy. Daddy got these for you. Just for you."

Heather grabbed Jack's hand and went with him to look at the pile of new clothes. "How about this one?" Heather asked as she picked up a John Deere shirt. Jack nodded his head yes. Heather helped Jack put on the clean shirt. Heather said, "These are cute, where did you get them?"

When she looked over to Bobby, she caught him looking at her with the strangest look. "Bobby?" She said his name.

"Oh, I got them while I was in Mitchell yesterday."

Mitchell? Why was he in Mitchell? Oh my god, Heather, quit this! Just ask him why he was there. Heather's mind was overloaded today, and she couldn't seem to stop it. "Oh, really, what were you doing in-" Before Heather could get the entire sentence out, there was a knock on the door and then a rush of people pouring into the house.

Jack seemed to panic– he reached for Heather's hand, "Mommy up." She reached down and pulled him up onto her lap. He snuggled into her arms. They were both content to sit quietly until these friends of Bobby's were settled.

There were several grocery bags placed on the kitchen table, along with a couple of cases of Budweiser. *Beer? And he is going into treatment on Monday?*

Many conversations were going on at once, someone was asking who needed a beer, another was telling a very animated story with a bunch of swear words and hand gestures. Everyone started to laugh. Heather looked for Bobby. He was coming from the kitchen with a big smile on his face, and it looked as if he was tucking in his shirt.

Jack reached up with his little arms and smushed her hands on either side of her face, "Mommy. Milk?"

He must have asked her a couple of times without her hearing him. Heather laughed, "Ok, buddy, let's go get some more milk."

At the kitchen table there were two girls, both had cigarettes lit and were drinking seltzer beers. Another girl had just walked out of the bathroom wiping something from her mouth. She said something to the girls at the table and they all started to giggle. One of the girls had short dark hair and was wearing a baseball cap, the other was heavy set with dark rimmed glasses, and the third, that had come from the bathroom, had long dark hair that was pulled up into a bun. She was a pretty girl, but her skin was blemished with scars and what looked like light bruises. Her eyes were dead, vacant. All three of the girls had on tank tops that looked two sizes too small. They kept talking, smoking, and drinking. None of them looked at Heather or Jack as she grabbed the milk from the fridge. Heather couldn't help herself; she checked the expiration date of the milk. *Ok, so this is good. A couple of days yet before it expires.* She went to the faucet. *Running water. Job must be going good.*

Heather was lost in thought when Bobby came into the kitchen. The small brunette made a move like she was going to stand up, but Bobby put his hand towards her signaling her to stay seated, she slumped into her chair and took a long drag on her cigarette.

"Hey buddy, are you ready to roast some marshmallows?" Bobby picked up Jack.

Jack started to whine a little bit and tried to fight being picked up. Heather said, "I'm coming too, Jack. Come on, let's go, it'll be fun." She headed out the back door. "Bobby, it looks like things are looking up for you."

She turned around only to see that they didn't follow her outside. She immediately panicked; she had just told Jack she would stay with him. When Heather went back into the house Jack and Bobby were nowhere to be seen and neither were the three girls who had been sitting at the table. The table itself was not even in the kitchen. She went into the living room, no one was there either. She heard loud talking and laughter coming from the front of the house. She went to the front door and everyone had gathered there before moving towards the bonfire that someone had lit around the side of the house. Heather thought to herself, *Ok, this is the Bobby I know.*

Bobby was standing in the middle of a group of people with Jack in his arms. He had them all enthralled with some sort of story about the new truck he was looking at and how he was looking for a matching kid-sized one for Jack. *This is where Bobby thrives, impressing people with shiny things and a version of his life that doesn't actually exist. A life of stability, honesty, and hard work. But this is the same guy who wants me to feel like I am a no one. The one who goes out of his way to gaslight me. This is the Bobby I hate.*

Heather was aware her mind was taking her to a very dangerous place, she knew these thoughts, unless controlled, would come out in the worst way. She wanted to march into the group and pull Jack from his arms.

"Hey, my name is Mike. You look pretty empty-handed. Can I grab you something to drink?"

An overweight man with long black hair that hung in his eyes was asking her if she wanted something to drink. Something from the past kicked in. Heather knew exactly what to do to get back at Bobby. All of his broken promises, lies, and horrible behavior wouldn't stop her from having a good time. In fact, didn't she deserve a good time for putting up with all of his bullshit? She lightly touched Mikes arm, "Yes, please. A seltzer drink, any flavor will be fine."

Mike came back with her drink awhile later and Heather stuck her hand out and said, "My name is Heather."

"You look familiar. Where do you work?" Mike replied.

"I actually work for a new non-profit, Walk America Clean. I don't think you would know me from there." Mike looked at her again, "Is it possible I would know you from the McDonald's in Winner?"

Heather laughs, "Possibly? I did work there a couple of years ago? I do go there every so often with my son." Mike did not look familiar to her.

"Ha! Ok, well we go there at least twice a week either for break-fast or lunch. Do you want to sit down at the table?"

Again, Heather knew she was playing with fire. "Sure."

Mike pulled out a chair for her. Heather sat and looked up to him and smiled, "Thank you."

As he sat down, he shook his head to the side which moved the hair from his eyes.

"So, who is we?" Heather asked.

"What do you mean?"

"You said 'we' go to McDonald's twice a week. Who is we?"

"Oh, yeah! I work for an electrical company in Winner. Our crew loves McDonald's. Fast, affordable, and friendly service." He recited the newest McDonald's ad. Both Heather and Mike laughed. Heather's drink was going down a little faster than she wanted, but she was finally starting to loosen up. When Mike asked her if she is ready for another she quickly said, "Why not?"

She stood up and looked for Jack and Bobby. Jack was playing in the dirt with some of the neighbor kids but Bobby was nowhere to be seen. She was fine with that. Heather sat back down in her chair and looked around her. For the first time since coming back to the reservation, she compared where she was now to where she used to be. Outside her apartment in Mitchell, she had green grass and a mature maple tree just outside her front window. Birds singing in the morning were her alarm clock.

Here, the ground below her was clay, there was no grass. There were no birds. There was a pile of trash towards the front of the road, it looked like someone had attempted to put it in garbage bags, only for the bags to be torn apart, trash strewn all the way down the road. Currently, the contents were being pilfered by two feral dogs, looking malnourished and unsupervised. Heather watched the older kids running in and out of the broken-down cars and trucks that were strewn around the yard.

What would her white friends think of all this? She was certain they would take it at face value. They wouldn't see the survival that laid beneath all of this. Mike came back with a seltzer for her and a Budweiser for him. She had to admit, she was liking this attention even if it was from a stranger. She reminded herself that just because she was relaxing with a couple of adult beverages, it didn't make her a bad person, a failure.

Heather couldn't believe it was already 5:30. She was having way more fun than she thought she would, as was Jack. He was taking turns riding bikes and making mud pies with the other kids.

There were now about 15 people at the party. Her new friend Mike was sticking close by except for the occasional times he disappeared, she assumed he was smoking pot, judging by the smell that came along with him whenever he returned.

Bobby and a couple of his buddies got the bonfire going. They had yet to roast any marshmallows, but the kids were having fun doing other things. Someone had yelled to the group, "Anyone want a shot?"

Mike looked at Heather, "You in?"

Heather wasn't feeling any effects of the alcohol she had already drank so she replied, "Sure." There was a voice in her head saying, *No. Don't do it,* but she again reminded herself one shot wasn't a big deal. She was an adult. And she hadn't done this for a long time. She had earned it. It was just one night.

Mike touched her arm and said, "I'll be right back."

Heather pulled her phone from the back of her jeans and clicked on her text messages. A message from Aunt Neen appeared, "How is everything going? Is Jack having fun? Is Bobby in a good mood? Home soon?"

Heather texted back. "Everything is going good. Jack is having a blast with the neighbor kids and I haven't seen a whole lot of Bobby. We'll stay for a while, don't want to take Jack away when he's having such a good time."

Before Heather could put her phone back in her pocket, she could see Aunt Neen was getting ready to reply.

"What do you mean you haven't seen Bobby? I thought the three of you were getting together to spend some time together before going back to Mitchell? I am confused... which doesn't take a lot nowadays. Ha-ha."

Mike returned with two shot glasses. Heather told herself she would text Aunt Neen back in a little bit.

She slid her phone into her back pocket and grabbed the shot glass. Mike raised his glass to hers and said, "To new friends."

She took the shot in one swallow. The fireball burned down her throat and gave her a familiar warm, heady feeling.

Part Two

"May His favor be upon you, and a thousand generations and your family and your children and their children and their children."

~ The Blessing, Cody Carnes, Elevation Worship

Chapter 12

Sheriff Dobson
August 2019

The dispatcher was speaking with the jailer through the walkie-talkie but their conversation was cut short because Sheriff Dobson had just entered the jail with Jack in his arms. The dispatcher went to take Jack, but he started crying almost immediately. Sheriff Dobson shook his head no and sat down across from the dispatcher's chair, holding Jack. He spoke with the dispatcher in a hushed tone over the sleeping child, "Thank you for running and grabbing those warrants from the judge."

Marlene handed Sheriff Dobson a cup of coffee. "No problem at all. It was nice to break up my evening a little bit." Marlene sat down at her desk and began to type. Looking away from her screen but still typing, she said, "Sheriff, do you know if the parents have anyone we can call for the little guy?"

"I did try calling Heather's Aunt Neen but she didn't answer. I left a message and texted her. That was roughly 15 minutes ago. You know, her Aunt Neen and I went to school together for a while back in Winner. She wasn't there for very long and then moved back here. She was always such a nice person." Talking to himself, Sheriff Dobson says, "Wow, what a crazy night. I'm surprised I was called in."

Marlene sighed, "We had three on duty tonight, but officer Haus was the only one that showed up."

"What the hell? Don't they need jobs? Don't they need the

money?" Marlene was aware Sheriff Dobson was asking a rhetorical question and remained silent.

"What do you think, Tom? Do we need to issue the parents with a TCD?"[17]

"With everything we found at the residence, and if we can't get a hold of a family member, then yes. There will also need to be an on-going investigation into this. I'm not sure we need to alert the feds but that may be the next thing that happens. I just can't believe it, Marlene, that these parents had no idea where their little boy was."

Marlene's phone rang. After a brief conversation, she hung up.

"They have Charlie Lawrence on her way. She is the FSS[18] from Mitchell."

A voice could be heard from the other side of the door that led to the cells. "Hey, Marlene, can you let me out for a minute? The door is broken from this side again." Marlene gave a little chuckle as she opened the door. Colter said, "My walkie-talkie isn't working again either and Heather is crying uncontrollably begging us to let her go." When Colter saw Jack sleeping, he lowered his voice. "She wants to know where Jack is. I have her crying and Bobby is yelling, telling her to shut up and that it was just a friendly argument. I told him the bruises on her face and fat lip tell a different story. He didn't like that. I think I need to tell him to grow a pai—."

Marlene held up her hand, "Whoa, Jailhouse Rock, remember we talked about this. Your job is to make sure they stay in their cell. No need to interact with them unless absolutely necessary."

Colter grabbed a soda from the fridge, "Yeah– yeah, easier said than done." Colter made a move to sit down in the other chair, across from Marlene. From the look Marlene gave him, he changed his mind and went back through the door. He yelled over his shoulder, "Can you make sure someone looks at this do—?"

---

17 Temporary Custody Directive

18 Family Services Specialist

The door shut and Marlene gave another little chuckle, "Man, I love that kid."

And just like that, Marlene was serious again, "So, it says here Bobby was just released from prison about six months ago. Heather had been good for about three years, probably because of this little guy." Marlene was shaking her head, "I hope they can figure out what they are doing." She pointed to Jack, "That little boy needs them."

It was four am, Sheriff Dobson was still cradling Jack as if he were a baby and not a toddler. He maneuvered Jack so he could check his phone again and take a drink of his just refilled coffee. *No message from Heather's aunt.*

When Charlie Lawrence from the Department of Social Services walked in, she was confused to see a big, burly man with a gray beard and mustache, Todd County Sheriff cap, and uniform holding a sleeping child.

Whispering, Sheriff Dobson said, "Every time I go to put him down, he starts crying. It's easier this way."

Charlie immediately liked Sheriff Dobson. She grabbed the chair sitting next to him and moved it so she was facing him, "I'm Charlie Lawrence. I'm the FSS from Mitchell. We haven't been able to get a hold of ICWA[19] or any family members. I noticed on our list of foster parents you and your wife are licensed. Would you be willing to foster Jack? In a couple of days, we can see how all of you are doing and see what happens with the case?"

The first night she cried the entire time. She was in a fog. Her brain was hazy from the alcohol and then the excessive crying. She begged the officer not to take her to jail. She pleaded with him to call her aunt. Heather panicked. "Please, please let me call my aunt and

---

19 Indian Child Welfare Act

just let me go home. I promise I will never do this again. Please!" The officer looked at Heather with pity and shook his head. "I'm supposed to be going back to school tomorrow. My son and me. Please..." Heather was sobbing.

The police officer grabbed her by the upper arm and pulled her towards the jail. As she entered through the doors, she couldn't breathe. She went through the steps of getting fingerprinted. Someone removed the shackles from her wrists and ankles and showed her to her cell.

Gray cinder blocks surrounded her. It was exactly what you see in the movies; a 7 x 8 room just big enough to hold a bed, small desk, chair, and toilet. A thin mattress lay on the wire frame bed. A flat, discolored pillow lay in the middle. She looked for a bible. What you couldn't tell from the movies was the rancid smell of the urine, and the Clorox they used to cover up the urine smell. The smell transported her right back to her first house with Bobby.

She was handed a pile of clothing and was told to change into the dark blue top and bottoms. Before doing so, she pulled them to her nose, hoping to find respite from the smell. *How is it possible even the clothes smell like urine and Clorox?* She couldn't think straight. She sat on the bed, not wanting to lay down, to give up.

Her mind kept going back over everything that had happened and what she could have done differently. She was so completely disgusted with herself; her thoughts were scattered, *Oh my God, what have I done? Here I am, Lord.* She didn't understand why those words came to her, but they gave her comfort and yet scared her at the same time. Her crying and moaning could be heard throughout the jail. *The least, the last, the lost... The lost... I am lost, Lord. It has been almost three years. Why am I here again? Can I be saved? Am I worth being saved? Who is telling Jack everything will be ok? Am I worthy of being Jack's mommy? Heather! Heather! Strong and able...*

She must have fallen asleep. When she woke, she was sitting against the wall with her knees pulled to her chest. Remembering where she was, panic threatened to overtake her again. Her eyes adjusted to the muted lights that were flickering from somewhere. Nothing hung on the block concrete walls. No one was there to tell her everything would be ok. She looked around again for a bible. No drawers for a bible to be in. No clock. *What time was it? How long had Jack been without her?* She folded into herself, again asking *Who is telling Jack everything will be ok? Surely Aunt Neen has gone to get him. Please God, please God, help us.* She was comforted. *Yes, he has Auntie.* She took a deep breath. She yelled for someone to tell her what time it was and she asked how long she would have to be in there. No answer. *Am I all alone? Does Jack even need me? Is he better off without me?* Her mind was doing crazy things. *Does anyone even care I am in here? Is anyone trying to get me out?* She knew it was insane, but she already felt forgotten.

Heather was lying on the bed with her back to the entrance of the jail cell. She had finally quit crying. She had no idea what time it was, but knew it must be early morning. Voices were coming from the other cells and from the office area. A coffee pot was humming or maybe it was a copy machine. She heard a shuffle of feet and a clearing of one's voice. She didn't move to look until he cleared his throat again, but louder. Heather tilted her head back over her shoulder. The young kid who was also the jailer the night before was standing at the bars. "I need to give this to you. Read it and let me know if you have any questions, please." Colter was trying to sound authoritative, but felt sorry for the woman.

Heather got up from the bed. Her head was pounding. She could tell the jailer wanted to say something but didn't. She grabbed the paper from his hand. It was a Temporary Custody Directive. The first thing Heather's eyes went to on the TCD was where it asked for the other custodian. *Why was it blank? Why wasn't Aunt Neen listed? Why wasn't she contacted to go get Jack? And then it said no other guardian available? How is that possible?* Heather could feel herself losing control. She took several fast, deep breaths, the tears started coming. "Do you know if I can call my Auntie?"

South Dakota Child Judicial System
TEMPORARY CUSTODY DIRECTIVE

NAME: <u>Jackson Bear Robe Windsong</u>

ADDRESS: ______________________________

MOTHER: <u>Heather Apalachia Windsong</u>

FATHER: <u>Bobby LaRouche</u>

Other custodian or guardian information: ______________

AGE: <u>2 1/2</u>　　DOB: <u>4/21/2017</u>

SEX: M <u>X</u>　F ______　RACE: Wh. ______　Ind. X　　Other: ______

DATE OF INTAKE: <u>August 10, 2019</u>　　TIME: <u>1:30</u> <u>AM</u>

CALLER: <u>Charlie Lawrence</u>

AGENCY: <u>CPS</u>　　PHONE: <u>605-999-9949</u>

MOTHER AVAILABLE: Yes ______ No ______
Suitable: Yes ______ No <u>X</u>

FATHER AVAILABLE: Yes ______ No ______
Suitable: Yes ______ No <u>X</u>

ALLEGATION(S): <u>Heather and Bobby were both arrested and transported to the Todd County Jail. They were both under the influence and unaware Jackson was taken from the home by male subject. There was extensive drug paraphernalia in the home. Once Jackson was located, no other guardian was available, so this leaves Jackson without a caregiver. He will be placed into DSS care.</u>

The jailer looked around and lowered his voice. "No, Ma'am. I am sure you will see her at court this morning."

"This morning?"

"Yes, Ma'am. That is why I had to deliver this document to you. To let you know the judge has ordered a hearing to decide who will watch your son while you are incarcerated."

The air left Heather's lungs. The room was closing in. Something was echoing in her ears. It was a howl or moaning. It wasn't until the young jailer opened her jail cell and walked her to her bed that she realized it was her moan. It was her own sound of the earth shattering. Her body was no longer hers. She folded into a ball of shame, disappointment, and hopelessness. A dull moaning sound still surrounded her and echoed off the walls. She must have fallen asleep because she awoke to the sound of her jail cell opening.

"Ma'am, it's time to go. I can give you five minutes but then I need to shackle you and get you upstairs." When Heather opened her eyes, she saw a clean set of dark blue pants and top and a toothbrush and toothpaste. Realizing this was the extent of the privacy she was going to receive, she quickly changed out of the jumpsuit she had on and into the new set. She swallowed her pride and used the toilet and quickly brushed her teeth.

Her reflection was not hers. The mirror had waves going through it, distorting her reflection greatly. She could see the monster she had become. Because they took her hair tie from her when she came in, her hair hung down her back. She ran her hand through it and wiped the sleep from her eyes.

She sat on the bed and folded her hands, first talking to Jack and then praying to God. *My sweet baby boy, mommy is so very sorry. Please, forgive me. Please, don't give up on me. Dear Jesus, remind me of your love and your promise. Dear Jesus, please wrap my baby boy in your arms and remind him I love him more than anything. Jackson, please don't cry. Mommy loves you.* Heather prayed the Lord's Prayer over and over. Every time her thoughts went to Jack, she would start to cry and would start lamenting all over again.

"Heather Windsong?" A deep voice came from the hallway.

"Yes?" Heather stood up from the bed and grabbed the paper she had received earlier.

The policeman that had arrested her the night before came around the corner. "Are you ready?"

"Yes. I am."

Sheriff Dobson unlocked her jail cell, "What size shoe are you?"

"7 or 7 ½."

Sheriff Dobson yelled into the hall, "Marlene, can you grab me some inmate shoes? 7 ½?"

Sheriff Dobson grabbed the shackles from his waist, "You aren't going to kick me, are you?"

"Of course not." In any other situation, Heather would have thought he was kidding. He brought her hands to the front and quickly shackled her wrists. After she stepped into the bright orange sandals, he shackled her ankles. Heather was humiliated.

"You can follow me." Sherriff Dobson stepped to the side while Heather stepped out. Heather jumped; the cell door slamming shut behind her. Once they rounded the corner, there were two other female inmates waiting for them. They were both in the same over-sized dark blue jumpsuits and orange crocs. Heather noticed they both had their hair pulled up with hair ties and looked very much at home here. They were both native as well. Heather put her head down. She didn't want to make eye contact. They may look the same as her, but that is where the similarities ended.

Heather met with her court-appointed attorney five minutes prior to her being called into the courtroom. She was introduced to Charlie Lawrence, the Family Support Specialist from Mitchell. She was trying to focus on everything they were saying, but she just wanted to see Jack. Once they both told her what would happen in court, they left the small room and walked into court.

She scanned the court room for Aunt Neen. *She has to be here, doesn't she?* Instead of seeing Aunt Neen, Bobby was brought in from the same back entrance they brought Heather through. He was in a dark, blue jumpsuit with orange crocs. Again, in a different situation, Heather would laugh at the fact that they matched. For a brief moment a smile drifted across her face. And then, like a punch to the gut, she remembered where she was and why.

Heather was being nudged by her attorney. He pointed towards Bobby. Bobby had been trying to get Heather's attention. He was mouthing the words to her, "I love you." Heather looked away.

Chapter 13

Shortly after waking up on that third day the jailer came in and told her someone was there to get her. The minute she stepped into the hallway and saw Aunt Neen, she started crying. Aunt Neen rushed to her and gave her a hug. "Wakanjeja,[20] I'm here now. We will talk at home."

Heather pulled away, "Where is Jack? Is he in the car?"

Aunt Neen didn't meet Heather's eyes, "Heather, we will talk at home."

"I don't understand! Where is he? Why didn't you bring him with you?" Heather was becoming hysterical. She had heard stories about how the native children would get taken away, never to be returned. *How is this happening to me? I promised myself this would not be my life.*

The jailer's voice echoed in her head. Heather was trying to focus on what the jailer was saying, something about a breathalyzer, three weeks, morning and night. She was handed a bag with her clothes and phone in it and was told she could change in the bathroom. At this point, she didn't care about anything except when she could see Jack. They walked to the car in silence and drove to Aunt Neen's without a word spoken.

The smell of sage met Heather as she stood just inside the door, numb. *Where is Jack?* Aunt Neen could read her mind and

---

20 Baby

immediately went to the stove to make hot tea. She sat down at the table, "Please, Heather, go take a shower and get some comfy clothes on. We do need to sort all of this out, but first, I want you to feel like a human again. Go."

Heather knew when not to argue and she did need a minute to catch her breath. The moment she stepped into the hot shower, she let out a deep, guttural cry. She scrubbed at her body, trying to erase the last three days from existence. *If I could just go back to that night and not go or leave the minute everyone else showed up. There were so many red flags. It was the alcohol. I know better. I know I cannot drink. Why did I? Why?*

She couldn't stop crying. Every time she thought about Jack; wondering where he was, it made her crazy. *Is he wondering why he isn't with me? Oh my God, I am going to lose my son, after one stupid night of drinking! I am going to lose Jack.*

As if Aunt Neen could sense when enough was enough, she came in and yelled above the sound of water and her crying and said, "Ok, time to talk."

While Heather was in the shower, Aunt Neen had set out a beautiful woven dream catcher and a pair of new slippers on Heather's bed. Heather put on a pair of sweatpants with a hoodie and grabbed the slippers and dream catcher from the colorful star quilted bed. "Thank you for the dream catcher and slippers." Heather choked on her words, starting to cry all over again. Any act of kindness from anyone, even Aunt Neen, was like a slap in the face. *God knows, I don't deserve it.*

Aunt Neen stood, pulled Heather into a hug and whispered, "This hug is meant to give you the strength of a thousand warriors and a peace in the creator knowing everything, all things, happen for a reason." Aunt Neen could feel Heather melt into her. The hug was working. Aunt Neen fought back tears. She hadn't cried yet over this entire situation, and she wouldn't now. Her niece needed her strength now more than ever. Aunt Neen gently pulled away from Heather, "We will get through this, but now, we must do the work."

Before sitting down at the table with her hot tea, Heather put on her slippers and hung the dream catcher in the window.

Aunt Neen started, "They haven't told me a whole lot about where Jack is, other than he is in the area and is with a professional." Heather knew what this meant; he was not with a Lakota family. "They did say that once you are out, you can call the DSS[21] office and they would go through everything with you."

"I'm confused as to why they didn't let him come here, with you, that night. Oh, how scared he must be." Heather was trying to hang on to any sense of calm.

Neen looked away, "Because it was so late and I didn't answer my phone, they had to take him somewhere."

"Will I get him back? Have I ruined our lives?" The last three days had taken their toll on Heather. Her eyes were swollen. She was pale and looked like she had lost weight.

"Of course, you will get him back! This isn't fifty years ago. DSS works with families to reunify. That is what their job is. If you can prove you are a good mom and that this will *never* happen again you will get Jack back. It will be hard work and they will be all over our business. But we know, it does not matter if we are Lakota, Chippewa, or the white man, if we cannot put our children above everything and everyone else, then we do not deserve our children. Easy as that."

Heather was shaking her head yes. Aunt Neen had her full attention. She continued, "Let's make a list of what needs to be done. Do not waste your energy for one more minute asking what if, we ask what now? What must we do now to get our boy back? That is our number one goal, and we will do whatever they ask of us."

"Oh, Auntie, what happens with my apartment in Mitchell? I need to call my landlord."

"I already called him. He is going to hold it for a couple more months. We need to give him a heads up when you want to go back."

---

21 Department of Social Services

Heather took a deep breath, "Do you think I can get my job back at McDonald's? I doubt Elder Miller will want me there. He is going to be so disappointed in me. I need to be doing something while I'm here and I will need the money." Heather turned her cup in circles. She whispered, "Oh my God, I am so embarrassed. How do I tell them what happened and why I want my job back after all this time?"

"You'll be honest. You will also want to have a conversation with Elder Miller. You will tell them you screwed up, but you have a plan in place. You will tell them you are not giving up on your dream, but for now your son has to be your main priority."

Heather jumped up from the table, feeling the energy her aunt was putting into the air.

She sat back down with a tablet and a pen. Together, they made a list.

1. Call McDonald's and Elder Miller to see if I have a job.
2. Get back into AA
3. Call DSS.
   a. When can I see Jack?
   b. What exactly do I need to do to get him back?
   c. Can they tell me anything about Bobby? (I don't want Jack seeing Bobby)

Heather paused writing, "Aunt Neen, not once have you yelled at me, even though I deserve the rage of a thousand white men. Why? Why are you so good to me?"

Neen hesitated, "Well, I know anything I could say, you have already said to yourself. I also know the good days we have lived outweigh the bad. I have no doubt you will be frustrated many times in the next several weeks and you will feel as if the whole world is against you. You need to remember they are not against you; they are against your behavior. Yes, you are Lakota, and because of that, you will need to work harder and fight like hell to get Jack back. That means when they ask you to do something, you *do not* argue. You watch your every action and your every word. They will look for any little thing to make this not happen. Don't give them the pleasure. My dear niecie, my sweet Ina, this will be the fight of your life. You need to make them see that the best place for Jack is with you and *no one* else. I know it and you know it. Now, you need to prove it."

CHAPTER 14

In a matter of one night, her life had come crashing down around her. And here she was five days later, trying to pick up the pieces. Heather thought the three days she spent in jail were the toughest part to get through. But finding out Jack was not with Aunt Neen, and having no idea where he was, was a hell no mother should experience.

At night her dreams enveloped her into a cocoon where everything felt normal. She and Jack were back in Mitchell. They were going to the park and daycare. He was with her wherever she went. And then her dreams started to fade, her reality holding her hostage and, once again, her tears started to fall. She lay in bed clinging to Hawkeye as if, somehow, he could transport her to Jack. As Heather lay there contemplating how she would get through another day, she heard her phone vibrate. Expecting it be Aunt Neen, she briefly looked at it, expecting to ignore the call. *She's calling to see if I have started anything on the list.*

Heather was surprised to see it was from a blocked number. *Great, Bobby?*

She sat up and steadied her breath before answering.

"Hello?"

"Hi Heather?" A woman's voice.

"Yes. This is Heather."

"This is Charlie Lawrence. We met at the temporary custody

hearing. I will be your case worker from here on out. I have information on when you can see Jack. Can you talk?"

Hearing Jack's name, Heather closed her eyes, sent up a quick thank you to her Creator, and gave Hawkeye a quick squeeze before jumping out of bed. She ran to the kitchen to find a pen.

"Yes. Yes, I can talk. Where is Jack? When can I get him? When can he come home?" Heather noticed a draft of cold air coming in through the front door. The lock wasn't working and, with any type of wind blowing, the door would pop open. She went to shut the door. Something outside caught her eye. It was a black sedan. It looked like someone had just shut the driver's side door. The windows were tinted. Just as she stepped outside to get a better look, the sedan pulled away. She stood there for a beat trying to decide if it was anything to worry about.

"Heather—are you there?"

"Yes, sorry. I'm here. When did you say I could see Jack?" Heather turned around, grabbed Aunt Neen's blanket and sat in Aunt Neen's chair, immediately feeling protected.

"I didn't say. What I said was we need to first talk about your case plan. I will be in Winner later this afternoon. Can you make that work?"

Heather was supposed to go in and talk to the manager at McDonald's at some point that afternoon, but all she cared about right now was getting Jack back.

"Yes. What time and where?"

They decided to meet at the DSS office in Winner. Heather pulled on a pair of sweats and her ACDC t-shirt. She pulled her hair into a pony and wore her running cap. She may not look the best, but she was comfortable.

Heather looked at the sign on the building: Department of Social Services. *Who was I kidding? What makes me think I can* be any different than anyone else? Wasn't it just a matter of time until I wound up here? Heather tried to quiet the hopeless thoughts that haunted her dreams, and now her reality. Everything she had heard throughout her life about this place taunted her mental state: Where families are destroyed. Once you step in, you never get out. The building that takes your children away.

Heather once again reminded herself to take deep breaths. Although she knew a quick and easy way to make herself feel better; she wasn't going to give up so easily. She was willing to do whatever it took for her to see Jack. She took a deep breath and pulled the door open.

Charlie was short. Heather didn't remember this. What she did remember was thinking Charlie was stuck in the 80's, with crimped long, blond hair and wearing blue eye shadow. But Heather could tell right away she was respected in the office, which meant she knew what she was doing. Although she was white and worked for the state, she said her sole purpose was to make sure their family stayed together. Heather believed her.

Remembering what her and Aunt Neen discussed the day she got home from jail and several times since, she was to make sure Charlie and everyone else knew how much she loved Jack. She was not going to give him up.

"I do want to believe you, Heather, but actions speak louder than words. According to the police report, there were drugs, guns, and all sorts of horrible stuff found in the home. The home that Jack was in. And the police report said you had no idea where Jack was? How can that be? Especially if you love him as much as you say?"

Heather couldn't believe what Charlie was saying! She began to cry, "That stuff was not mine! I told the cops the same thing! Why doesn't anyone believe me?"

"So, you are saying you knew where Jack was? And you let Mike take Jack? Because if that's the case, why didn't you tell the cops that right away instead of making them go on a wild goose chase?" Heather knew this was all true, yet she couldn't believe they were talking about her. If Charlie was phased by the tears, she gave no indication. Instead, she reached across to her other desk, grabbed the Kleenexes, and sat them in front of Heather.

"Go ahead and take a minute. I'll be right back." Charlie grabbed a piece of paper and left Heather there alone.

Leaning back in her chair, she took a couple of deep breaths and remembered what she learned in AA. *You are the best mom for Jack. I know it and you know it. Now you have to prove it.* Heather could hear Aunt Neen as if she was sitting right there with her. Heather took a deep breath and reached for another Kleenex. She wiped her eyes and blew her nose.

As Charlie walked into the office, she held out a bottle of water to Heather. "Here, take this."

Heather grabbed it and took a big drink, "Thank you."

"No problem." Charlie flipped the sheet of paper in her notebook, "Now, let's start again. Who is Nana?"

"Nana is my Auntie Neen. She has raised me since I was six. Jackson calls her Nana."

"Ahh, ok. Yes. He keeps asking for Mammie and Nana. I am assuming Mammie is Mommy?" The air was knocked out of Heather. She quickly grabbed another Kleenex and let the tears fall. All at once, she was sick to her stomach. She thought she might vomit. She wanted to run from the room, run from this horrible nightmare she was in. She was crying for Jack, Aunt Neen, and her dead parents.

All of a sudden, she was a six-year-old little girl. *Where are my parents? Why did they leave me? Don't they love me? Mommy! Daddy!* And then she saw Aunt Neen there, holding her as she cried. First as the abandoned six-year-old and then so many times after that. The most recent one, when Heather stepped out of jail. *Oh God, please don't let me do that uncontrollable sobbing thing I do, where I can't even talk. Heather, get a hold of yourself.*

"Ok. Ok." Charlie jumped up from her desk and grabbed the other chair adjacent to Heather. "Actually, Heather, this is a good thing for you! The fact that Jackson misses you both is a great thing. It tells all of us he loves you both and we will be able to tell the judge that." She stood up and grabbed her laptop from the other side of her desk and sat back down scooting her chair closer to Heather. "Here, this is the case plan we will be working through." She turned the laptop so Heather could see everything.

"So, I need to have all of this completed before I even see Jack?" Heather was preparing to collapse in hopelessness.

"No. You need to have these things done before Jack comes back home. You can see Jack as early as today. I have already talked to the foster parents and they said to let them know what time and they will drop him off at the visitation center. So, the faster we get through this, the sooner that happens. Let's talk a little bit about Bobby. You are no longer living with him? I don't have his file in front of me, but I think he was kept in jail on a parole violation.

Heather dried her eyes and with a strong voice said, "No, Jack and I moved out two weeks prior to that Saturday. We were staying with Aunt Neen until we could get back to Mitchell. At this point, I don't want Jack to see Bobby without supervision. Bobby knows people, on the inside and on the outside. And I especially don't want Jack to have to go to the jail to see him."

"Ok. No, we wouldn't allow that at his young age. However, if Bobby does get out, and even if he doesn't, we may have to set up visitations at the Visitation Center for them. As Jack's dad, Bobby does have rights. That is something I can look into." Charlie scribbled some notes on a notepad. She took a long swig of her energy drink, leaned back in her chair and said, "Ok. Let's get a visit lined up with your baby. Sound good?"

Before Heather could respond, Charlie was already punching in a number to the phone.

After her meeting with Charlie, Heather stopped to talk to Aunt Neen at the MMIW office. She briefly filled her in on how everything went at DSS and told her she was going home to change. When Auntie didn't reply or even look up, Heather knew she had something else on her mind. She could barely see Aunt Neen behind all of the boxes that were on her desk, "What is going here? Why all the boxes?"

"We had a cold case come back up. A disappearance that happened about 10 years ago. A young mom and her little boy from Valentine went missing on HWY 18. Sad, sad deal. Gone. Without a trace." Neen took out a document and highlighted a portion of something on it. She put the document back into the folder and looked at Heather. "This case is definitely reminding me; things can always be worse." Neen sat back in her chair. "Ok, tell me why are you going home to change? I think you look just fine."

"Charlie arranged a visit with Jack at the Visitation Center. I'm going to put that soft shirt on that Jack likes to snuggle into. Also, Charlie said it would be a good idea to take him some things that remind him of home."

"He is going to be so happy to see you."

"I'm nervous." Heather sat on the edge of her chair across from Aunt Neen.

Neen shoved a box over to the side, so she had a better view of Heather. "I'm sure you are. You are probably feeling a lot of things. Just remember, he loves you very much." Aunt Neen was looking at a framed picture of Jack from his first birthday on her desk. "I am sure he is so confused as to what is going on. Ina, you must be strong. And don't let him see you cry. It will confuse him even more." Neen walked around the desk to Heather's chair. Heather stood up and Aunt Neen pulled her into a hug. Heather could hear Auntie's voice crack. "Give him a big hug for me."

"I will." She gave Aunt Neen a peck on the cheek and said, "Anyway, wish me luck. Love you!"

"Good luck, Ina. Love you more."

The visitation center was hard to find. It was hidden at the end of a dead-end road on the outskirts of town. The address wasn't listed anywhere online. Had Charlie not given it to Heather she was not sure how she would have found it. The visitation center was also a part of the safehouse for those finding respite from domestic abuse.

Sitting there now, in the parking lot, Heather felt even more nervous than she did when she was with Aunt Neen. She looked down at her clothes. Jack's favorite shirt, her best blue jeans, and her Hey Dudes. She wore her hair in a long, thick braid that hung down the middle of her back. She was wearing a little bit of makeup. She pulled the dream catcher from the rear-view mirror and held it. *Please, Creator, protect us and show us your mercy.* Instead of putting it back, Heather put the dream catcher in her bag with the other things she brought for Jack. The car door gave a little squeak when Heather opened it. She could hear the muffled sounds of a softball game from somewhere nearby. The September air was crisp but still warm. She was immediately transported back to last September when she and Jack were invited to the church potluck in the park. They had a softball game going on at the same time and everyone was happy, laughing and cheering.

"Hey there, I think someone is waiting for you." Heather was brought back to the present by a kind stranger pointing to the window at the front of the visitation center. Heather looked in the direction he pointed and saw her little man in the window. Heather smiled and looked to the man and said, "Thank you." The man was already in his car and didn't hear her.

Although Heather couldn't hear Jack, she could see him saying the word over and over, "Mam! Mam!" She ran to the door. "Mam!" Heather could hear her baby yelling for her the minute she opened the door. "Mam!"

Heather quickly signed her name on the registration log and followed the worker back to the visitation room. The minute she stepped into the room Jack ran to her arms. Heather threw her bag to the floor and picked him up into a bear hug. She buried her face in his neck and breathed in his baby smell. *Thank you, Creator, thank you, Lord, for this second chance.*

Heather whispered to Jack, "How am I going to leave you? I am so sorry, sweet baby for what I have done. Please forgive me. How is it possible it has been four days without seeing you and snuggling you?" *I am breathing again. Finally, I am breathing!*

The worker told Heather she would be outside the room and to let her know if they needed anything. Heather sat down with Jack on her lap.

The visitation center was not as bad as she had been told. It was a 10 x 12 room, brown carpet with light brown walls. There was a tub of toys in the corner that looked out of place. The room had a huge mirror on one side and directly across from the mirror was a kitchen area with a small table and microwave on the right and a changing table on the left. And although the mirror made the room look bigger; its true purpose was to closely monitor every single movement in the room.

Every movement was written down and recorded to be played many times over. Anyone who encountered the case would watch and re-watch the recording, dissecting every look, word, and move-ment, making note of how Heather reacted when she saw Jack and, more importantly, how Jack reacted when he saw Heather.

Cases that involved babies looked at many things. Do the par-ents know how to make a bottle or how many ounces of milk the baby should have and at what temperature? When does the baby get burped? Do the parents know what the different cries mean? How fast does the parent react when the baby cries? How much or how little is the baby held?

Jack scrambled off Heather's lap and went to the bag she had brought in. Heather sat on the floor with him. She grabbed the bag, "Yes, let's look!" Heather couldn't wait to show Jack what she brought him. Today, along with a children's book about puppies, Heather placed a family picture of her and him with Aunt Neen and Hawkeye inside the book.

Jack grabbed the picture, and pointed to it and said, "Nana."

Once again, Heather held back her tears, "We will see Nana real soon! She misses you soooo much!"

Heather knew she and Jack were being monitored but she didn't care. She was just so happy to be there with him. Heather opened the children's book and Jack sat on her lap. She grabbed his blanket from her bag and he snuggled into her. She started reading the book, but when she came to the words, "And I love you very, very much," her voice cracked. She stopped reading. She put the book down and squeezed him into another bear hug.

She sat with him and he continued to snuggle into her. She said over and over, "I love you, baby. Mommy loves you so much." She felt tears starting to run down her cheeks. Would she ever forgive herself? Jack pulled away and brushed a tear away with his finger. That made Heather cry even more. Jack started to cry too and handed her his toy car he found in her bag. Still holding Jack, she got up and grabbed a Kleenex. She sat back down, wiping Jack's nose and then her own. She said, "Ok, enough crying, I need to hear about all of your adventures." Jack started talking, much of what he said she didn't understand but she played along and he continued to talk.

Heather was happy to see they hadn't cut his hair. He was dressed in khaki shorts and a short-sleeved Paw Patrol shirt; clothes she didn't buy for him. Hair she didn't comb for him. She tried to reconcile her feelings of knowing he was being taken care of, but taken care of by someone else and not by her.

He tugged at her hand to go over to the tub of toys. She lost track of time trying to forget where they were. It seemed like only a half hour had passed when the worker came in and told her they needed to start packing up to leave. Heather shook her head yes and started to silently cry again. She wasn't sure she could do it. *I honestly do not know how I am going to walk out of here without him. He won't understand. I am his mommy. I need to be with him, he needs to be with me.* Heather felt herself start to panic, her breath leaving her again. Heather heard Aunt Neen in her head reminding her, "You must be strong for Jack. Think of the long-term goal. Don't let him see you cry too much. That will make him sad and even more confused."

Heather grabbed Jack's sippy cup from her bag and handed it, along with his blanket and book, to the worker. The worker smiled uncomfortably, knowing what was coming. She tried to make it sound fun for Jack, "Hey, Jack, should we go look out the window and watch mommy go to her car?" As the worker started reaching for Jack, he started crying and ran to Heather. She picked him up and he buried his head into Heather's neck.

"Jackson, you need to go back to the Dobson's. Mommy can't go with you yet. I love you so much. I will see you again in two sleeps! Mommy loves you so very much."

She shoved Jack into the worker's arms and turned and ran to her car. Right before the door closed, Heather heard Jack wail, "Maaaammmm!" Heather could barely see the car door handle through her tears. She couldn't handle this feeling. She was losing her mind. She needed to let it out somehow. She grabbed her cell phone and punched in the number of one of her old friends. She sent a quick text.

Are you around?

Wow! Long time no text, chica! I am out of town picking up floor samples. Be back tomorrow.

Heather knew 'floor samples' was a code word for whatever drug he was running low on. Heather hesitated before texting back.

Is anyone else around that can help me?

Not today, Chica. I will call you tomorrow.

She couldn't wait for tomorrow. She needed to dull this pain. She wanted to feel better, even if it was only for a little bit. Her only other option was to find someone here in town. She knew just the place.

As she looked up from her phone, something caught her eye. It was Jack, he was still looking at her from the window, tears rolling down his cheeks. She was so busy trying to score a hit, she didn't even notice her little boy sitting in the window wondering where his mommy was going without him. Heather talked out loud as if Jack could hear her.

"Don't cry for me, sweet baby. I will figure this out. I need you more than I need these goddamn drugs! I know that. Please, don't cry for me." Heather buried her face in her hands. When she looked back up, Jack was gone.

Heather put the car in drive. She knew exactly where she needed to go.

CHAPTER 15

The running path Reyna chose today was one that followed the train tracks into town. Occasionally she would see the train coming over the bridge to the west. If the sun was positioned just right, it looked as if the train was coming out of the sun. The trail led her down to a plank bridge that ran over a stream from the Jim River. She knew when she got this far she had reached her halfway mark. She continued to the big ash trees that provided her with some much-needed shade. Feeling her phone vibrate, Reyna grabbed it from her leggings. She didn't want to stop the adrenaline rush she was having, but she also knew she was told to answer her phone if it rang. So, begrudgingly, she slowed to a walk and answered her cell.

Seeing the caller ID, Reyna quickly answered, "Hi, Beth!" Beth was Reyna's supervisor, she had trained Reyna and assigned her to her first case as a CASA. The respect Reyna had for Beth was like none other.

"Hi, Reyna, how are you doing?" Beth always seemed to be smiling and happy. Reyna could hear it in her voice over the phone. Reyna also knew when Beth asked, "How are you doing?" She really wanted to know.

Reyna gave her a brief synopsis of how the family was. They talked a bit about the online bible study they were both participating in and agreed that they were enjoying it. When there was a slight pause in the conversation, Beth explained to Reyna what her call was about, "I have a young mom who has lost her way. She has a little boy who has come into foster care. Because you have had experience with the littler kids in the past, I thought of you right away in maybe being the CASA for this little guy? If you think you are interested, I can tell you his name and those associated with the case. As you know, we want to make sure there is no conflict of interest."

Reyna closed her last case over two months ago and was hoping to be assigned to another one. Reyna said, "I'm interested."

Beth went through the names of the family members. No conflict of interest. They were good to move forward. Reyna asked, "So, this is a Native American family? Where is the case located?"

Beth hesitated, "Yes, I probably should have mentioned that. The case is in the Winner area. Most of the court hearings will be in Mission, or Todd County Courthouse. Now, there are times where we can possibly attend court from the judge's chambers in Mitchell, using video. But, for the first couple, I would plan to attend in person." Beth continued, "Also, I would ask that we travel together for this case." Without saying too much, Reyna understood what Beth was saying, domestic cases hold large amounts of emotion. Domestic cases on the reservation even more so. It was best for them to use the buddy system until they could get a better handle on exactly what the case would entail. Beth continued, "I would also suggest as soon as you can, to reach out to the mom. She seems to be open to working with DSS; the dad, not so much."

"Who is the DSS agent on the case?"

"Charlie Lawrence."

"Ok, great! I can touch base with her."

"Yes. I do think it would be a good idea for you to reach out to her and get her opinion on things."

"Ok, sounds good. I have worked with her in the past, I'll add her to my list of calls to make."

Before hanging up, they arranged a time for Reyna to come into the office to pick up the file. Reyna was already thinking about the case and praying for all those involved. She clicked her phone back to her playlist and slid her phone into the pocket of her leggings. How fitting, "God is on the Move" was playing. She felt a sense of peace come over her. She had two miles to go. Reyna set off to finish her run so she could get back home in time to start supper.

Following supper that night, Reyna looked at her watch and decided to give Charlie a call. As she gathered her notebook and pen, she sat down at her desk, reflecting on her relationship with Charlie.

Friendships are tested every day and Reyna firmly believed your oldest friends are your best friends. Every day communication is not needed, and sometimes it takes a tragedy or a triumph to bring friends back together. That is how Reyna felt about her friendship with Charlie Lawrence.

Ten years earlier they were young moms taking on the world in their careers and families. They met through their kids for the first time at the tumble gym. It didn't take long; soon they were sched¬uling play dates, coffee times, 5 o'clock social hours, and outdoor runs. They were best friends. Then, life happened. Charlie's daughter went into gymnastics. Reyna's daughter stayed in cheer. Charlie went through a divorce. Reyna went on to have two more kids focusing her attention on her family. However, even though they weren't as close as they once were, Reyna still attended Charlie's mom's funeral and Charlie still sent flowers to the hospital when Reyna's daughter was having her tonsils removed. They knew each could be called upon and the other would show up.

Reyna was looking forward to working with Charlie on this new case. She dialed Charlie's number.

"Hey girl, what's up?" Charlie greeted Reyna just like always. Reyna smiled.

"Not much. This is a work call so if you want me to call back tomorrow, I certainly can." Reyna was aware of how protective the

DSS workers were of their time; if they weren't careful, this job could overtake their lives.

"I'm good. I just finished supper. Maddie is with her dad and now I am relaxing with a High Noon, thinking about jumping in the hot tub. What's up?" Charlie had just changed into her swimsuit. She held her phone between her ear and shoulder as she tied her knee length terry cloth robe around her waist. She opened the sliding glass door and waited for Nookie, her Lachon puppy, to follow her out to the deck. The fragrance of lilies and petunias greeted her. The twinkling lights warmed the cool night and gave that vacation vibe she loved. It was the perfect September night that invited a relaxing soak in the hot tub. Her red and white petunias lined the deck railing and her lilies sat in the center of the patio table.

Looking around her deck, she was thankful she had spent the time and money making it her outdoor sanctuary. Going through her divorce several years ago, she thought it was the worst day of her life. However, that divorce, and the split proceeds from the house sale, afforded Charlie her dream home and the outdoor living that came along with it. She turned on the hot tub to warm up and sunk down into her oversized wicker chair as she drank her daily dose of Vitamin C from her grapefruit flavored cocktail.

Reyna spoke, "Well, that sounds like a great night! I will try not to take up too much of your time. I'm calling about the Windsong/ LaRouche case. Beth called me earlier today and I thought I would get your thoughts on it before I reach out to the mom and dad."

"Ah, ok! I am pretty sure it will be a quick case. I put her through the wringer when I met with her yesterday."

"Did you make her cry?" Reyna knew the answer even before she asked the question. Charlie had told Reyna years ago that she had a certain protocol she used when meeting with her clients. She needed to know right away how serious they were about wanting their kids back, and if they were willing to do the work that was needed.

"Maybe a little." Charlie hesitated, "Ok, quite a bit. Right now, she seems very focused on getting her son back. But, of course, it's like every other case. She needs to stay away from the drugs and other bullshit. I am not sure she can do it." Charlie took a drink of her grapefruit High Noon. "I truly hope she can. The Dobsons are the foster parents and they say the little boy, Jack, cries for Heather and his grandma constantly. "Heather didn't say a whole lot about Bobby, other than she doesn't want Bobby ever to be left alone with Jack. She wouldn't go into detail."

"Is he wanting to work with us?" Reyna hadn't met too many Native American men who were willing to leave the chip on their shoulder at the door. She also had only met one who was able to get clean. Alcohol and drug abuse were so prevalent, it was destroying their reservations. However, Reyna wanted more than anything for little boys like Jack to know it was possible to grow up to be a strong, successful, Lakota man.

"I don't get it. Why do these Native American women allow this to happen to them? What is the pull? And don't say generational trauma. I am so sick of that phrase! They claim we are destroying their culture, no, we are not." Reyna had a tendency to jump around on topics, especially when she was fired up about something she believed in. "They are destroying it themselves."

"Don't you think that's even changing though? I feel like they are finally starting to see that they also have power. Their voices mean something. More and more of the women are moving off the reservations." Charlie got up to let Nookie back into the house. Before sitting back down, she grabbed a bottle of water from the fridge, "Out here, they know they have a voice and they will be protected. Now, if they could just figure out how to stay sober. If they could do that, they could rule the reservation, if not the world."

"You know what, I do agree with you. I have been seeing a few success stories on Facebook and the news about Native American women who are turning their lives around. I love seeing it and I want it to continue. How do we help going forward?"

Reyna heard the TV flip on in the other room. She looked at her watch. They had been on the phone for over 20 minutes. She had ten more minutes or her family would start the movie without her.

"By doing what we are doing. And acknowledging the breakdown between us and trying to strengthen it. You know, Heather was clean for about two and a half years, yes for nine months of that she was pregnant, but her baby was born healthy and not addicted to drugs. That says a lot right there. Heather was also enrolled in school in Mitchell. I think this one might be one of those success stories. Maybe this was a case of one and done?"

In Charlie's 17-year career, she had seen only a handful of cases where the case closed and she didn't see the same actors come through the system again. And, in those cases where they fought and won, they were coined as the elusive one-and-dones.

"Really? You think so? Is Bobby still in jail? Has she been in contact with him, do you know?"

"Yes, yes, and no. Yes, she has what it takes. Yes, he is still in jail. And no, she has not been in contact with Bobby. I verified with the jail as well on that. Heather said she doesn't want anything to do with him. And she does not want to do visitations together. Oh, and by the way, Heather had a visit with Jack yesterday. She didn't know it, but I was there. There is no doubt she loves that little boy. I have seen a lot of visits, this one actually tugged at my heart. I didn't think that was possible anymore." Charlie laughed, but they both knew how sad it had become that truly meaningful moments were few and far between. And most times, those moments were so fleeting they wondered if they had happened at all.

"And you mentioned Jack is in foster care? There was no next of kin?" The last two cases Reyna was a part of involved children from the reservation, no family members stepped forward to help with the kids.

"Actually, she does have an Aunt Neen, who Jack refers to as his Nana. However, the cops couldn't reach her that night. So, they called me and thank God I had noticed the Dobsons were foster parents before, he was one of the cops on duty that night."

"Wow! That worked perfectly! I plan to sit down and read the file tonight after the kids go to bed. I'll let you go. Enjoy the hot tub and I'm sure we'll talk soon." Reyna felt a little stab of jealousy. How nice it would be to relax in a hot tub with peace and quiet.

"No problem! Have fun with the kiddos! Talk to you later!"

Reyna jotted down some notes from their conversation, she then wrote on a sticky note: 'Enter into database' and stuck it to her laptop screen. As if on cue, as she closed her laptop, she heard the words from the other room, "Mom! We're starting the movie!"

Chapter 16

Reyna Moore
September 2019

Reyna gathered her notes. She was preparing herself to call Heather for the first time. The introductory call could give so many clues as to how the case would go. Reyna was also careful not to assume too much right off the bat. She muted her TV and punched Heather's number into her cell phone. She put it on speaker phone.

"Hi Heather, this is Reyna Moore. I am a Court Appointed Special Advocate, or CASA, here in Mitchell. I'm wondering if we could set up a time to meet?"

"Who is this?" Heather sounded confused and her speech was somewhat garbled, Reyna was wondering if she woke Heather from sleep.

"This is Reyna and I have been given your case. I've been appointed by the courts to be an advocate for your child. I do my best to meet with all parties involved and give my opinion to the judge on where I feel the child will thrive."

Heather was talking very slowly when she said, "Oh… yes. Charlie said this may happen. So, what do I need to do?"

Reyna was not surprised to hear some confusion from Heather. Chances were that since having her child removed, she had been inundated with people from the police, DSS, attorney's offices, all trying to set up times to meet with her. Reyna was hoping her voice was relaying the patience and grace she was offering this young momma. "Well, I would like to meet with you as soon as possible. When would be a good time and do you have a place in mind?"

"How about the McDonald's in Winner?"

"McDonald's works great. Which day are you thinking?"

"Umm, maybe Friday?"

"Friday works great. Is there certain time that would work best?"

"Maybe over the lunch hour?"

Reyna was writing everything down. She repeated the details back to Heather, "So, this coming Friday at McDonald's in Winner and should we say 12 pm?"

"Actually, I just remembered, can we do 10:30 instead? I work at 11:30 that day."

"Ok, do you work at McDonald's?"

"Yeah"

"Ok, great. 10:30 it is. The number I just called you on is my cell number. Please text or call if something comes up before then."

"Sure." Heather's voice was flat.

"Ok, sounds good. See you then." Reyna hung up the phone. She saved Heather's contact information into her phone. She also made a mental note to check if someone could ride along with her to the visit. She wasn't holding her breath on Heather showing up. Reyna got the impression that Heather was only half listening. These meetings could go either way. Reyna hoped Heather came to realize sooner than later that the only one who could make this situation better was her.

Adventure seemed to be calling out to her. And so, today, she listened. Reyna guided her Yukon XL onto Highway 18. Rolling green hills painted the landscape. Among the hills were clusters of huge, green trees. The sky was fighting for the canvas as it hovered in brilliant blue. The tall sage grass and wildflowers covered the ditches. This was certainly God's country.

Out here it wasn't tough for her to imagine living off the land, to imagine a simpler life. In fact, she always thought if she had had a past life, it would have been during the 1800s. Horse drawn wagons seemed to appear before her eyes. And knowing she was coming into Indian country; she could visualize the teepees and the Indians running as free as the wild horses. *This has been a beautiful drive so far and it really is just so peaceful here.*

Reyna was driving the same route Heather would have taken back and forth to Mitchell before this all happened. It was important for Reyna to try to understand Heather, exploring and studying her way of life was one of those ways.

As Reyna continued to drive, she noticed a stark difference in the houses and the land. It was as if the clay was starting to swallow up the lush, green, rolling hills. The peace she had felt before was slowly changing into a feeling she couldn't immediately identify.

At right around the 10-mile city limit sign, she began to see the poverty that was so prevalent. Trailer houses with no foundations, sitting on lots with no grass, just brown clay; several with no windows or windows that were boarded up. The houses were like abandoned shacks that littered the beautiful South Dakota landscape. There were multiple cars sitting everywhere on the properties, most looked like they were broken down or being worked on. Many of the houses had toys outside, Reyna couldn't believe kids lived here.

She realized, for the last several minutes, she had been praying her car wouldn't break down and for a brief moment she thought perhaps she should have brought someone with her. The condition of the houses brought out so many emotions, including horror, sadness, and a sense of loss. Loss for this culture, loss for the innocent children born into this. *And if I was from here? Wouldn't I feel shame and embarrassment? Oh my God, I sound like a spoiled white woman!* Internally, Reyna made a point to check herself. She knew one of her biggest downfalls was judging others. *Judgment is the last thing they need.*

The feeling she couldn't identify earlier? Hopelessness. Not just fear, sadness, and loss, but that feeling of complete hopelessness.

In some of her CASA training, Reyna remembered the statistics of this area being incredibly stark. The suicide rate was at an all-time high with roughly 177 suicides attempted between January and mid-August last year. Something like 60% of residents lived below the poverty line. And no wonder they were suspicious of us coming in to help, as there was a 22% chance of their children being removed from their families and placed in foster care.

Reyna remembered sitting in on that training and deciding right then and there she wanted to be a part of the solution in helping this culture thrive. These were the places that were never talked about among the politicians and media. It was as if the Indian reservations in South Dakota had been forgotten. These places have the most rapes and incest cases per capita in the nation, and yet we never hear about any of it.

Reyna thought about a mission group she had been researching earlier in the week. It was a work group that went in and donated time and resources to helping fix sagging porches or weatherizing homes in the area. They enticed you into serving by saying, "You will see the Rosebud Reservation as an exciting world of rolling grassy hills and deep, tree-lined creek bottoms." Reyna was trying hard to see that side of the reservation.

As she came closer to the town of Mission, the grade school and university greeted her at the city limit. Both buildings were a drastic change from what she had just seen. They were brick and beautiful, flanked by wide sidewalks and green grass. They begged you to give this place a chance. Unless you had been in the buildings, you wouldn't know they had security guards that worked at every entrance and metal detectors the children had to walk through every day to enter the buildings. The university offered housing on campus; however, the campus shut down every night prior to dark with strict orders to not be walking around during certain hours. The graduation rate was 8%. How can these children be expected to do well in class when they are up against such challenges? *What makes these generations not only want to stay here, but to live like this?*

With these drastic statistics, Reyna couldn't help but wonder: *Who are the heroes here?*

Reyna arrived at the McDonald's a few minutes early. She was dressed casually with her curly dark hair pulled back in a low pony, she had taken the front portion and braided it back off of her forehead. She brought out her notepad and double checked if her pens worked. After talking to Beth about the logistics of the meeting and the fact that they were meeting in Winner, not directly on the reservation, they agreed Reyna was fine to go by herself.

Now that she was here, she was a little nervous. She kept looking at the front door waiting for Heather to arrive. It was now a little after 10:30. *I will be bummed if she doesn't show up, but it also wouldn't be the first time I was stood up by one of my cases.* Just as Reyna thought this, Heather came from the back. Immediately, Reyna was struck by how beautiful she was. She had on her work shirt with nice black pants. Her hair was raven black, pulled back neatly into a single braid. She had a golden-brown complexion with dark brown eyes. She had on a little makeup which accented her dark eyes, making her look almost Asian rather than Native American. As Heather approached the table, she brought her hand out to shake Reyna's, looking directly at her. *Well, she has passed the first test, just by showing up.* Reyna was trying not to show the shock on her face. *Is this the same girl I spoke to on the phone the other day?*

Heather quickly said, "Sorry I'm late. I came in early to get a head start on inventory and had to explain a few things to my coworkers."

"No worries at all." Reyna said

Heather asked, "Before I sit down, can I get you something to drink?"

Reyna replied, "No, thank you, I'm good."

"Ok, great, I'll be right back." Heather was quickly back with a coffee, notepad, and pen. So far, Reyna was completely impressed.

"Thank you for meeting me." Reyna started the conversation.

Heather said, "I wouldn't have missed it. I'm hoping you can help me so I can keep my baby."

Reyna picked up her pencil, leaned forward, and said, "Well, you meeting with me is a very good start. Can you tell me in your own words how you and Jack got here?"

Reyna was now home in her office, preparing to go over the notes she had taken earlier. The two-hour drive back gave her time to think about everything she had seen on her drive to Mission and heard from Heather, and how she would approach the next steps in this case. She opened her laptop, brought up her CASA database, and read through the police report again. She was always amazed how something written in black and white could be the furthest thing from being black and white. She was looking forward to making a call to Heather's aunt. Reyna made an additional note to reach out to the Dobsons, the foster parents. This would also give her an opportunity to meet Jackson.

The one phone call Reyna was not looking forward to was to Bobby. She made a note reminding her to contact the jail where Bobby was staying. *It probably wouldn't be a bad idea for me to confirm all of the transformations and revelations Bobby supposedly has had while in prison.* Reyna sent over a quick email to Beth, first telling her briefly about her meeting with Heather and then asking her to send off the appropriate paperwork to the jail so she could access any and all records. Reyna completed her notes in the database, glanced through her appointments for the rest of the day, and decided she had just enough time to get a run in.

Chapter 17

Charlie couldn't believe how perfectly this was working out. She had been on this case less than two months and it seemed as if everything was falling into place. She had just sat down to visit with Sheriff Dobson and his wife. The more she got to know them, the more she liked them. Shirley Dobson was a retired teacher, so she was more than willing to help take Jack to visits with his mom and dad. And Tom was just a big teddy bear, although you wouldn't know it until you got to know him. He was a big guy; Charlie would guess him to be 6'5 and around 280 pounds.

The three of them were sitting in their three-season room. Shirley was an avid plant lover; she had all varieties decorating the room. The plants were well placed and paired with the wicker chairs, creating an extra homey feel. The white French doors leading out to the patio allowed the sun to shine through and warm the room naturally on this cool, October day.

Shirley had placed an iced tea in front of each of them, and took her seat next to Tom and across from Charlie.

Charlie asked, looking at each one of them when she said their name, "Sheriff Dobson, Shirley, if it's ok, I would like to take some notes while we talk?"

"Please, call me Tom, and of course."

"Yes, absolutely." Shirley said.

Picking up her cellphone, Charlie made sure it was on silent. She picked up her pen and notepad and started summarizing the facts of the case. "I have noted the visits have been determined to be separate as this was a request from Heather. Bobby is pushing to have family visits, but Heather is adamant she doesn't want that, and she has requested the visits between Jack and Bobby be monitored. They have set up visits to be at the family services center in Winner, however, the mom visits will eventually be moved to her Aunt Neen's house, where Heather is living." Shirley nodded in agreement.

"We'll talk about visitations in a minute but, for the most part, how is Jack doing?"

Charlie looked at both of them. Tom and Shirley looked at each other. Tom said to Shirley, "Go ahead, honey."

Shirley appeared to tear up a little bit, "Jack is a joy! He has finally started to sleep through the night; however, it takes him awhile as he still cries every night for his mom and his Nana. It breaks my heart." Shirley had short, white, curly hair and piercing blue eyes. She took great care with her appearance; her nails were perfectly manicured with a bright pink polish. She had on a lipstick color to match. She wore glasses that were attached to a very fashionable chain. She removed the glasses and, as if by magic, pulled a Kleenex from the sleeve of the blouse she was wearing. Charlie noticed the sleeves of the blouse were rolled up just a little at the ends, this allowed for her gold watch and gold chain to appear as she dabbed the tissue to her eyes.

Charlie was very much aware of how close Jack was to his mom and grandma, but that couldn't take away from the fact that there was a very good reason they were not here right now. This type of circumstance was so difficult. When going to school and choosing this as a career, they warn you of these types of scenarios, and how hard it could be to stay neutral. Charlie decided to move the conversation in a different direction.

"OK, let's talk about visitations. How are visits going? Let's start first with dad."

Shirley gathered her composure, "Jack is inconsolable when we go there. I absolutely cannot leave the room without him scream-ing. Bobby appears to take it in stride. During the last visit, Bobby demanded I leave the room, so I did. After ten minutes of Jack screaming, he knocked on the window and said to come get him. As I was leaving with Jack, Bobby yelled something about making sure I fed him, as if saying Jack was hungry and that is why he was acting that way. Jack also is a different kid after those visits, he doesn't want to leave my side. He pulls at his hair and refuses to lay down for nap. He will fall asleep in my lap, but I cannot lay him down or he will start screaming. I really don't like the fact that Bobby comes in the jail garb. Thank goodness they bring him early so Jack doesn't see the handcuffs, but it's almost as if Jack just doesn't want to be there with his dad."

Writing furiously, Charlie paused, looking up from her notepad. "I'm going to make a note to come and watch the next visitation. Also, before I forget to tell you, the judge has requested a CASA be appointed to the case. Her name is Reyna Moore and she will be calling you in the next couple of days. You will love her. Now, tell me about the visits with mom."

As Charlie reached for her iced tea, Shirley smiled. "It's bit-tersweet, the visits with mom. He loves going there, but he hates leaving. It rips my heart out every time. Heather is trying so hard. Her Aunt Neen is also a big help to her. I just hope she can stay away from Bobby; he has a way of getting under her skin. Heather is always there when we get there. She always has something for Jack like a toy or a book. She looks healthy. She is a very pretty girl and you can tell she loves that little boy more than anything. She acts strong in front of Jack but the other day we had left his book inside, so I ran back in to grab it and she was all out sobbing. I am not sure if it helped or not, but I did give her a hug. I told her she is doing a great job and that we are proud of her. Oh, and another thing, Jack loves his dog, Hawkeye. In fact, we are thinking we need to get a dog around here." Shirley looked at Tom. Tom smiled. His smile reached his eyes every time. They were a wonderful couple. Charlie was happy they stepped up for this family.

"Charlie, is there any way we can go down to one visit a week with Bobby? We are more than happy to continue taking Jack twice a week for Heather, but we really think the visits with his dad are just too hard on him." Shirley was holding her breath.

"I was kind of thinking the same thing. I'll need to discuss this with my supervisor. I'm thinking if we get any pushback from Bobby, we would need to back off on that idea. But I can always ask." Charlie made a note about the visitation. Shirley let out her breath and sank into Tom.

Tom leaned back in his chair and crossed his legs, "Do you know how much longer we will have Jack? We love having him, but we have plans to go visit our daughter in Utah over Thanksgiving and were just trying to figure out the details."

Charlie made another note about the Dobsons taking a trip and them possibly needing respite if the case was still going.

"I really don't know for sure. I know the court is requiring some things of the parents to do to make sure Jack is safe if, or when, he is returned home. The last thing we want is to see this little guy in foster care again, which, unfortunately, is normally what happens. However, I have made a note to find respite care for Jack during your trip, if that works for you."

"That works just fine." Tom agrees.

"Also, how are you guys doing on gas vouchers and grocery vouchers?"

This time Shirley answers. "We're just fine with those."

"And do you feel safe enough to keep taking Jack to see his mom on the reservation?"

"Oh goodness, yes! In fact, I am looking forward to seeing Heather, Aunt Neen, and Jack interact with each other. Jack has a very different life there than he does here. But that is his mom and grandma and he loves them and wants to be with them. I want that as well, for all of them."

Once they were done talking, Tom called the babysitter and asked them to come home from the park. Charlie wanted to make sure she saw Jack before heading back home. It wasn't much longer and she could hear some commotion coming towards them. Jack ran straight to Tom. Tom picked him up and put him on his shoulders. Jack giggled and giggled, which made everyone laugh.

While everyone was being entertained, Shirley stepped out of the room to pay the babysitter. Soon she was back, and she helped Jack down from Tom's shoulders. "Hey buddy, did you have fun at the park?" Jack shook his head yes. He looked at Charlie and backed up towards Shirley. He started tugging at his hair.

"It's ok, Jack." Tom said. "This is Charlie and she is here just to visit and to say hi. She is just getting ready to leave."

Charlie did not move towards Jack. She could see he was very nervous. *These kids interact with so many people once they go into foster care. From the police to the social workers to the lawyers to the counselors, it's never ending.*

Right then it came to Charlie, "Hey, Jack, can you tell me all about your puppy, Hawkeye?" Jack took off running towards the other room. Well, that didn't work the way I wanted it to. Jack came back in holding a picture, *Yes! It did work.* The picture was of him, his mom, Aunt Neen, and Hawkeye. He backed up to Charlie, still holding the picture. She reached down, picked him up, and set him on her lap. He went through the picture and pointed at each of them and, in his little toddler voice, said their names. When he was done, Jack jumped down and ran to Shirley, putting his hands up. She picked him up and snuggled him.

Charlie smiled at him and said, "Jack, thank you for sharing your picture with me." Charlie would take this as a huge step in earning Jack's trust. She didn't push it. She gathered her notepad and pen and put everything back into her bag. She stood up and said, "Thank you, to you both, for welcoming me into your home. Please don't hesitate to call me or email should you need anything. I will plan on coming by next week, same time and day if that works for you?"

Tom started walking towards the door, "I'll be at work, but Shirley will be here. That should work for you shouldn't it, hon?"

Shirley stood up with Jack in her arms, she set him down on the couch and handed him a blanket. He cuddled in and seemed content, still holding his picture. Shirley met them out in the entryway and said, "That will work just fine. We have visits set up with his parents the day before but maybe we can get those switched around to have all the visits on the same day? It would be more convenient and, I think, less stressful for Jack." Charlie shook her head yes, while telling herself to make a note in her notepad to look into that. "Yes, and, either way, I will see you at some point next week. Thanks again."

As soon as Charlie got out to her car, she took out her phone, notepad, and planner. She put a few things into her planner and wrote some notes about her visit. She also put a reminder into her phone to check on switching the visitation day next week. She had two more visits to complete before her day was over. She checked her messages and missed calls; entered the next meeting address into her maps on her phone, and slowly backed out of the driveway.

Chapter 18

Reyna Moore
October 2019

She pulled into the gravel driveway; the house sat just a block from the elementary school in town. It was a light blue house with dark trim. It was modest but looked like it was in good condition. Before Reyna could knock, the door opened.

"Come in, please."

Reyna would soon find out that Aunt Neen was a force to be reckoned with. She was full of wisdom and spoke in English most of the time but also threw in some Lakota words when she needed emphasis. She wore a little lipstick that gave her a pop of color with her short dark hair. She wore black framed eye glasses that made her look very serious. It was her brightly colored clothes that gave away her spunky personality.

Her house was tidy and cozy. There were books sitting next to the chair with a handmade blanket draped over it. From where Reyna stood, she could see at least four dream catchers, all made with brilliant colors. Reyna could smell some type of herb in the air, it gave the home a very calming feeling.

"You're smelling sage." Neen smiled, "Can I get you a cup of tea?" Before Reyna could answer, Neen went to the kitchen and brought back two cups of tea. "Please, come sit down and tell me, how can I help you?"

Reyna could see where Heather learned her manners. Neen walked to the couch in the living room. Reyna was drawn to the chair with the blanket. Neen moved the books a little and set the tea down on the end table next to Reyna's chair. Reyna shifted the chair just a little so she was more in eye contact with Neen.

"My name is Reyna Moore and I am a CASA. Have you heard of what we do before?"

"Just from what Heather has told me."

"Ok. Well, I am here advocating for Jack and Jack only. I don't work for DSS, the police, or the tribe. I volunteer as a CASA, which means Court Appointed Special Advocate. And although 'court appointed' is in the name, think of me as an impartial advisor." Reyna took a sip of her tea and moved to the front of her chair. She was fighting the urge to wrap the blanket around her. Not because she was cold, but because she felt so at home here. Ironically, sitting here reminded her of when she was a child at her grandmother's house. She reminded herself she was not here to make friends, she was here on official business. "The judge felt it was necessary to have an unbiased opinion, or witness, to determine where Jack will not only be safe in his environment but also thrive in his environment. My purpose for visiting you is because Jack talks about you all the time and Heather has mentioned that this is where her and Jack come if they need a place to stay. Can you tell me how you think Heather is doing and what you think the future looks like for her?"

"I love that girl and her little boy more than anything, but I worry I have lost her." Neen took a deep breath, "When she was pregnant with Jack, she fought so hard and still continued to fight. She is such a good person. Why is it hard for our young girls to understand they can do it on their own? When she needs help, I don't mind her asking me. I want her to ask and I want to help. If it comes down to her depending on me or an overly hyped-up dipshit named Bobby, I want her to depend on me."

Reyna stifled a chuckle at Neen calling Bobby a dipshit. Neen continued, "I have had the opportunity to see many other places. I have volunteered with the Navajo Nation– the area I was in was remote and beautiful. There was no crime there. We were an hour and half away from any big city. I was able to work with amazing people with amazing ideas. That is what I want for my reservation. I came back from that trip with big ideas. And yet, I get back and I do what I can, but the culture here is a tough one to change, but I am still trying."

Neen shook her head slowly as if trying to shake a memory loose. "Ok. Let me get back to my precious niecie. She lost her parents at a young age. But, overall, she had a good upbringing. Her and I had a bond from the very beginning. I believe our creator planned us from the beginning. He knew we needed each other. There isn't anything I wouldn't do for her."

Reyna pulled no punches, "Why don't you have custody of Jack? Did DSS call you when they picked him up that night?"

Neen took a deep breath, "They did."

Reyna looked at her expectantly, "And so?"

"I made the decision that this was not my battle to fight. You have to know, I struggled with it. I have witnessed what happens once DSS gets involved. However, it was a chance I was willing to take if it helped my niece wake up. By me getting involved, it would have made it too easy for Heather. She knows they tried calling me. But I told her I was sleeping and didn't answer. It would destroy her to know that I told Tom to do what he needed to do. I will tell you right now, the minute this is all over, I am packing her and Jack up and they are going back to Mitchell. You know they were supposed to leave the next day for Mitchell?" Neen didn't wait for Reyna to answer. "She had finally reached her breaking point. She wanted to leave; Bobby didn't know she was leaving. He asked if Jack could go over and spend a couple of hours, but Heather didn't want him going over there by himself." Neen's voice dropped to a whisper. "Yes, this will always be our home but this place holds too many spirits from the past. The long ago past. It is not my niece's job to keep those spirits company. Not anymore."

Before she continued, Reyna asked, "Has Bobby ever lived with you?"

"No, he was going to when he was released from jail, but he ended up finding a place at the last minute that he moved into for awhile. Heather was adamant she didn't want him living here. After he came back last April, he lived with a friend for a short time before moving to Mitchell with Heather. These past few months have been a roller coaster." Neen's voice was reflective. She had a way of talking matter of factly, but with a sense of urgency. Reyna could tell she had many thoughts going through her head. Reyna remained silent and let her talk.

"I will be the first one to admit, our systems, ours here on the reservation and yours there in white man land, they make it nearly impossible for someone to get back on their feet after being released. Especially someone like Bobby. He has no family left. He and his friends still carry the burdens of our peoples' past. And, for some reason, those burdens are hard to put down. They have no money. The only place he knows is this place. After he moved to Mitchell, for a while, I believe he was really trying. I believe he loves Heather and Jack. But I also believe he just doesn't know how to let the past go and if he can't do that, then he is of no use to anyone. He and Heather have been through so much together. You know, they were best friends in their teen years. They were inseparable. She loves him but she is embarrassed by him too. I don't think Jack should be around Bobby and I have said that from day one. I know Heather wants Jack to have a real family, but that real family will not be with Bobby. He doesn't have it in him. Now that he has tasted the devil on his tongue, he won't ever rid of it. That is a fact."

"What is the relationship like between Jack and Bobby?"

"Again, Bobby loves Jack, but Bobby loves his misery more. He drinks and does drugs; it makes his depression worse. He becomes a different person. Even at Jack's young age, he knows how to read Bobby's moods. And, really, isn't that the saddest thing?" Neen asked the question to Reyna, not expecting an answer.

She continued, "Jack's job is to be a kid, a happy-go-lucky kid.

He shouldn't have to worry about not having food to eat or getting sick from drinking rotten milk in the refrigerator. And he surely should not be worried about the people coming into his home and whether he is safe. Honestly, when I think about it, it makes me want to scream. Can he not see the waphethokeca[22] he has in front of him? Can he not see the second, third, countless chances he has been given?" Reyna was aware that Neen was in one moment talking about Jack, and then switched to Bobby. "Heather tells me many things, but I know there is a lot she hasn't told me. You know the phrase, what you don't know won't hurt you? Do you also know how many times that has been proven false?"

It was 3:00 pm, Reyna had just switched her laundry over and looked at her watch. She had just enough time to throw that night's meal in the crock pot before she left to get her daughter from school. Suddenly, her phone started to ring. Reyna looked at it. The number came up as a blocked call. Although normally she would never answer a blocked call, today she did. An automated voice came on prompting Reyna to accept a call from an inmate, then there was a brief moment of silence followed by Bobby's voice saying, "Bobby." As soon as she heard Todd County Jail she rushed into her office. Before she could change her mind, Reyna accepted the call. When she heard the call click over, she concentrated on sounding professional.

"This is Reyna."

"Hello?"

"Hello, Bobby. Thank you for calling me."

"Yea, sure."

Reyna had several thoughts going through her mind. *Did Heather ask him to call me? How did he get my number? If he is in*

---

22 Miracle

prison, can he hurt me from there? Would he hurt me? She knew these thoughts were irrational, but she couldn't help it. She took a deep breath and said, "How are you?" *Shit! Why would I ask that? Of course, he is not good, he is in jail!*

He chuckled and said, "Happy, happy."

"That's good." *Oh my God, get it together, Reyna.* She felt frantic. She grabbed the first piece of paper she came across on her desk and opened the center drawer and grabbed a pen.

She wondered if he sensed her nervousness, before she could say anything, he said, "I'm calling to see what the situation is with Jack. Why do I only get one visit a week now? And why is he always crying at our visits? Is Heather saying shit to him?" *Ok. So, I know now why he is calling.* Reyna hadn't seen Bobby before. She had definitely tried looking him up but didn't find anything on social media. Reyna immediately started to jot down notes.

September 25, 2019; Bobby called me – 3 pm

Strong, clear voice

Asking why Jack cries at their visits?

"Those are both really good questions. I am not sure why your visits went to once a week. I'm also not sure why Jack cries. That is something we can ask the DSS worker." Reyna was trying to remember her CASA training and wanting to make sure Bobby was feeling heard. She purposefully repeated back to him, so he knew she was listening.

"Speaking of DSS, have you been in contact with Charlie?"

"No, not really. I'm getting the impression no one cares about me. I'm doing everything I'm supposed to be doing–but for what? My probation officer tells me I may not get out for a while. I also think it would be easier to have Jack come here for visits rather than me having to be transported to the visitation center? Can you check on that?"

Asked if he has met Charlie — would like to meet more?

Frustrated — doing everything he should — can probation officer tell him when he is getting out?

Bobby had a strong Native dialect, when he talked it was as if his jaw was clenched and he held onto his words too long, making them sound like an 'e' sound. She sensed a change in him, as if he went from hopeful to hopeless. Reyna tried to guide Bobby back to some of the questions she would like answered.

"Bobby– I can make note of these things and follow up with Charlie and have her call you. But, can I ask you a couple of questions?"

"I guess." His reply was flat.

"Do you know what it is I do? As a CASA?"

"Not really. Only you're supposed to help us."

"I'm actually appointed to the case by a judge but that is where the interaction with the court stops, other than giving my report to them. I advocate only for Jack. I tell people to think of me more as an impartial advisor. I meet with each and every person in his life to determine where I think the best place would be for him to thrive. I don't work for DSS, the judge, the state, or ICWA. I am here only for Jack."

"Ok."

"Can you tell me in your own words how you think you got to this point?" Reyna always liked to see how, and if, people took responsibility for their actions.

"What do you mean, how I got here? Heather was in one of her moods, making me all jealous and shit. She always know what she do'in to me."

"Ok, but why are you still in jail?" Reyna did not appreciate the woe is me dialog.

"When I was arrested this last time, I was still on parole from my drug arrest a couple years back."

"I see. So, do you know when you will be released this time?

"I have to go back to court. Not only for this case but judge will make me show for a parole hearing."

"Are you doing any counseling?"

"They keep say'in I'll start soon. I was suppos'd to the other day, but another guy in here got in my face and made me miss my appointment."

"Have they told you when your next appointment will be and who the counselor you will be seeing is?"

"No. They don't tell me noth'in here until it happens."

"Okay. Do you know the date you are supposed to get out?"

"Nah."

"Okay. Do you want steady visitation with Jack once you are out?"

"Yeah! Heather and I are go'in git back together and give Jack a good life."

"Again, that is something we need to ask DSS. Okay. So, I would like to see you start counseling right away. Also, I would like to ask you to make two lists, more for yourself than anyone else. The first list will show everything you have done since being in prison to improve your future. The second list will be the top three things you will have as priorities once you are released. Remember, the judge will need to see action, not just words, when it comes to the safety of Jack." Reyna would love to believe everything Bobby was saying, but she couldn't. Not yet.

Ask Heather — Getting back with B?

Didn't B tell her he was doing counseling?

Ask PO — Is he getting into fights?

"Ok and if I do all of these things, I will-" Just then Reyna's phone beeped, *Shit! It's the school!* She looked at her watch. *Shit! I'm late again!*

"Bobby, I need to go. I'll be in contact again, I'm sure. Thanks for talking with me." She clicked over to the other line and grabbed her car keys off the desk while saying, "I'm on my way! Sorry!" and hung up. She wasn't in the mood for a long, drawn-out lecture about how her kid depended on her. She knew.

Chapter 19

Family court was held on Tuesdays in Mitchell. Charlie and Reyna agreed to meet at the local pub for a quick bite of lunch prior to court to get caught up on their mutual case. They decided on the pub for a couple of reasons, it was close to the courthouse and it provided them with a level of privacy where they could speak freely while keeping the conversations confidential.

The pub sat at the south end of Main Street. In the old days, when it was first built in 1909, it was part of the Chicago Milwaukee and St. Paul Railroad, it carried passengers and freight for over 40 years. It was renovated in 1990 to become the beautiful restaurant it is now. In the early restaurant days, it catered to the college crowd, now families and business-minded individuals were the norm. Many of them were hoping to feel the nostalgia that an old train depot could offer, especially if you were lucky enough to be dining while the train came through.

Charlie had blond hair and blue eyes and was naturally skinny. Reyna had dark hair and dark eyes and had to work for every skinny bone in her body.

Both women were acutely aware of the imaginary line that divided their friendship and their roles this case involved.

Because Charlie worked for DSS, her ultimate goal needed to be reunification of the family. And because Reyna was a CASA, she advocated for the children, or in this case, the child. Charlie and Reyna had great respect for each other. Charlie attended four years of school to do what she did, Reyna was a volunteer. Each considered what they did to be their mission in life, their calling. This was the third case they had been on together. The first case was five years ago and they had disagreed to the bitter end. Reyna was fighting for the kids to be adopted by foster care and Charlie was fighting for the kids to be returned to their biological mom.

And although they met occasionally to discuss different aspects of a case, today, as usual, both were guarded on what they shared. They started with small talk. Reyna remembered seeing Charlie's daughter winning the All-Around at State gymnastics, "Can you tell Maddie congrats for me with winning All-Around?"

Charlie smiled, "Yes, I will. And what about Kate and her cheer team? Looks like they are rocking it as well!"

Now, it was Reyna's moment to smile, "Yes, they just returned from Florida. Tough competition, but they had a blast and saw a lot of great teams."

The waitress came over and took their order. She filled their water glasses and walked away.

"So, how do you think Heather is doing?" Reyna cut right to the chase.

"Good." Charlie took a breath as if she was going to say more, but remained quiet.

Reyna realized she would not be able to 'lead the witness' today. Charlie was too smart for that. Reyna stated what was on her mind. "This is my opinion. Yes, Heather is doing what we ask of her but are we doing too much handholding? Can she do these things without us reminding her, taking her to her appointments, and following up with her? What happens if in six months she is reunified with Jack and she is unable to follow through?"

"First of all, this case is completely different than the first one we were on together. Heather has a support system, a job, and goals. She has already demonstrated she is a great mom. She has just made some poor decisions. We cannot determine the future; we can only go with what is in front of us right now, and give her the tools she needs for when she is doing this on her own again."

Reyna continued, "I went to go see Jack at daycare. The hair pulling hasn't gotten any better. The daycare provider said that when DSS comes to transport him to a visit, he begins to whimper and they have to bribe him with food. Now, it could be Jack is on to them and just knows how to work it for more food, but the daycare provider thinks there is something else going on. I went and met with Heather and I've talked to Bobby, he did ask me to ask you about a couple of things - don't let me forget - and I did have a really good visit with Aunt Neen. I'm not going to lie; I was a little nervous going to the reservation by myself. I wasn't prepared for the devastation I saw."

Charlie was shaking her head in agreement, "Yes! I've been there. It's definitely not what we're used to as far as what homes look like around here, but it is definitely a loving home. Heather loves that little boy with her whole heart, as does her aunt. As far as Jack pulling at his hair and whimpering when he leaves for visits, that could be any number of things. Is it that he is seeing Heather or the fact that right after visitation with Heather is the visit with dad? Remember, Reyna, I am there during most of those visits. He cries when he has to leave his mom and it breaks my heart every single time. We need to reunify those two. My mind is not made up yet on Bobby."

Reyna was not satisfied. "I still have so many questions. She mentioned to me that she is having issues with her car. She also told me she has tried many different drugs in her past. Can we trust that she won't go back to that? Are they going to start random drug testing? How is she going to afford raising Jack? Also, Charlie, Jack is really happy with the current foster home and they have said a number of times they would be willing to adopt."

"Are you kidding? We are nowhere near thinking Jack needs to be adopted. I don't want to bring anything up to Heather about adoption."

"Of course not." Reyna agreed.

The waitress brought over their food and refilled their water glasses. Charlie pulled out her planner and asked Reyna to fill her in on the conversation she had with Bobby.

Reyna Moore

Reyna was scrolling through her phone, looking for a cool video she had seen on cascading succulents. *Ha! Found it!* She was sitting at her dining room table in front of the bay window. Carefully she set her phone up against one of the pots for easy viewing. After she gathered the succulents together she put on her gardening gloves. Just then her phone rang. It was Beth. *Perfect! I want to tell her how great this case is going.* Reyna pulled off her gloves, grabbed her phone and pushed the green button.

"Hi Beth!" Ready to settle into a nice conversation, Reyna put her phone on speaker and set it back down. She pulled her gloves back on and brought the succulent close for inspection.

"Hi Reyna. I just got a call from Bobby's attorney. Bobby called him very upset. He said he wants you off the case. He said you talked to him on the phone and you hung up on him when he asked you about being able to visit Jack when he gets out?" Beth said the statement as a question.

Reyna's stomach dropped. She was very confused. She thought the phone call between her and Bobby had gone well. Getting up from the table, she pulled her gloves back off, and carried her phone into the office to find her notes. "Give me a second, I'm heading back into my office."

"Sorry to bother you."

"No big deal at all. I am confused though; I thought the conversation went really well."

Her desk was full of miscellaneous papers. Between helping with her husband's business and her regular job, the desk often looked like a bomb went off. She remembered grabbing a piece of paper and making notes on it. But, of course, now she couldn't find it, and, of course, she hadn't entered the conversation into the database yet. She moved different piles around. *Here! I found it!* She turned it over and it said United Way on it. No wonder it was hard to find, this paper was from a conference she had attended months ago. "I found it!"

Reyna read through her notes. She silently cursed her horrible handwriting, which she attributed to being left-handed. She looked at the time of day he called her. 3 pm. She remembered the call, but why did he think she hung up on him?

"Beth, I remember I had to go get the kids from school and I had to cut the call short, but I didn't hang up on him."

"Ok. He also said he thinks you are just out to take his kid because he is native. Did you say anything like that to him?"

Reyna's blood began to boil, "No! That didn't even come up. Seriously, Beth, I am so frustrated! Of course, I want what is best for Jack! It wouldn't matter if he was purple, red, or green. If you can't take care of yourself, how are you going to take care of your kid? I didn't say that to him, but I was thinking it. I will upload my notes tonight so you can read them. Sometimes I wonder why I'm even doing this."

"Because you have the best heart and you want the best for Jack. We don't do this for the parents, we do this for the children. Believe me, this conversation his attorney relayed to me doesn't sound quite right. It sounds as if nothing is his fault and he is doing everything he needs to be to get out early for good behavior. His attorney was skeptical because when he called and talked to the jail, Bobby had gotten into a couple of fights and refused to attend any counseling."

"Ok. I am going to make note of that. When I talked to him, he made it sound as if he was trying to get into counseling. I will shoot you a text once I have my notes uploaded. I haven't had a chance to call the jail yet. I, too, wanted to confirm some of the things he told me." She ended the call with, "Thanks for calling me, Beth, and sorry you had to deal with this."

"No worries at all. I will continue to pray for everyone involved."

"Thank you very much." Reyna hung up her phone and immediately went to go type in her notes. She wouldn't be able to enjoy the rest of the evening knowing this needed to be done. She also added the conversation she just had with Beth. She saved them and uploaded them. She fired a quick text over to Beth, grabbed her gardening gloves from where she had hastily dropped them earlier, and headed back to the table. Plant therapy was exactly what she needed.

Chapter 20

Charlie Lawrence
November 2019

The court room was on the third floor, it smelled of old cigars and dark, mahogany wood. The walls were lined with paintings of distinguished, past judges. The bailiff sat just inside the door and the court reporter sat a few feet from the witness stand. Directly in front of the judge was Heather and her attorney, Bobby's attorney, the State's Attorney, and the child's attorney. In the galley sat Aunt Neen, Charlie, Reyna, the Dobsons, and a representative of ICWA. The one person not present? Bobby.

As if the judge was thinking the same thing, he looked at Bobby's attorney, "Mr. Hayes, where is your client today?"

"Well, your honor, that is a very good question." Mr. Hayes, the young court-appointed attorney, maybe in his late 20's, was flipping through a manilla file folder. He had on a cheap brown suit that looked like he had slept in it. His plump cheeks flushed with the entire court's attention focused on him. Charlie knew she was being hard on him as, like her, he was probably living out of his car and eating on the road five days out of the week. He slumped his body forward onto the table with his hand on his forehead and looked at the judge. "I believe there is some confusion as to where my client is right now. I was thinking he was still being held here in Todd County, but he may have been transferred because of another pending case?"

The judge looked to one of the clerks, "Barb, can you check on this for me and let me know following court? For now, we will proceed. But, for future reference, Mr. Hayes, you may want to check with your client prior to attending court."

"Yes. Your Honor."

Charlie was sitting in the Todd County court room, willing herself to focus on what the judge was saying. She appreciated this little mix-up this morning, it created some excitement to an otherwise standard court hearing. Today was one of those days she was thinking of everything else she could be doing. She was the DSS for three cases here in Todd County. She needed to be here by 9 am and after the two-and-a-half-hour drive, and having already sat through three hours of court, paying attention at this point was a struggle. She thought to herself: *Honestly, I don't get paid enough for what I do.* She was instantly mad at herself. How many times did she have to remind herself how great her life was compared to the kids she was helping? Yes, she was tired of constant court dates, constant paperwork, and the constant running. But she knew the reason she did all of this: the children. For the children who had been taken from their homes, their parents, their life; the only life they had ever known.

And for a majority of the kids she had helped, many never got to go back home. Instead, they were adopted out or shuffled from foster home to foster home. Unfortunately, 15 more kids from the reservations just came into care. Charlie had studied extensively the historical trauma amongst the Native American population. She understood the challenges they faced and how it affected today's children. She was reminded to stay diligent in helping these parents. Her focus needed to be keeping these families together, against all odds.

Charlie grew up in a Baptist home. Their summers were spent on family camping trips and mission trips. The relationship she had with her sister and parents was one she wished for all children to have in their lives. And those mission trips gave her the vision of making the world a better place. In fact, her daughter was about to the age she was when she went on her first mission trip. Charlie made a mental note to check on mission trip opportunities through her church for Maddie to attend.

"Ms. Lawrence, you have a couple of comments you would like to make? Now is your chance." The judge peered over his glasses and looked directly at Charlie.

Charlie was brought back to the present. She jumped to her feet, notes in hand. "Your honor, in light of mom starting counseling, remaining separated from Bobby, and maintaining a positive support system, we ask the court to review again in two months. If things go as they have been, we may be looking at reunification just after the first of the year."

Her eyes scanned the court room. Charlie was always amazed at the number of people that were brought in for just one court case. Judge Jones looked at his computer screen. He took a deep breath and said, "It is my understanding that we are all in agreement that mom is taking the steps DSS is asking her to take?"

He looked at each of the attorneys and called them by name. One by one they all said, "Yes, Judge." Judge Jones looked directly at Heather. "I am going to schedule a review hearing two months from today. If Mom continues to make good decisions, it is quite possible we can close this case."

The judge was one of Charlie's favorites. He treated each case, and the members involved, with dignity and respect. He truly wanted what was best for the children. "You have made some very poor decisions in the past and your little boy deserves better. You have been attending counseling on a regular basis, please continue. You have completed your parenting classes and, for that, I am grateful. You have also been able to maintain a good job and have built up a great support system, some here but also some in Mitchell. These are all wonderful strides, but you are not done. As a mom, you are never done. Your work must continue. Do you understand?"

Heather nodded her head, "Yes, Judge."

Judge Jones looked briefly at his notes, "Also, from this point forward, Heather, you are to be very selective on who you decide to give your time to. You have a big goal in front of you and this may be the hardest fight of your life. As the old saying goes, 'If you are not part of the solution, then you are part of the problem.' Leave the past in the past. What is done is done. You can't go back. You can only look ahead. I encourage you to take this time and really figure out who is in it with you for the long haul. I am giving you permission to make some tough decisions and to hurt some feelings, if needed. Remain steadfast in keeping your family together. Your decisions now will either have positive or negative consequences for generations to come."

As the judge spoke, he made eye contact with every person in the galley finally resting on Heather again.

"Yes, Judge." Heather looked at the judge and then quickly looked down.

Charlie, once again, was so impressed with Judge Jones. He was thorough and fair. His cases usually lasted longer than with other judges, but that was because he took the time needed to make intelligent assessments. He knew the weight of his decisions and what they meant for these families. Charlie looked at Heather, it looked as if he was getting through to her.

Following court, Charlie, Reyna, and Heather decided to meet in a side room off of the courtroom to discuss the next steps. This was the second time Reyna had met with Heather face to face. Reyna was really happy to see Heather doing much better this time around.

Reyna held out her hand, "Nice to see you again, Heather." Heather shook Reyna's hand awkwardly.

Charlie said, "Ok, the reason I wanted us to meet is so that we can make sure you stay on track." Charlie did not mix words and looked directly at Heather. Heather was looking down at her hands.

Charlie pressed, "Do you understand what I am saying, Heather?" She pulled out a chair and sat close to Heather.

Heather looked up and said, "Yup."

Charlie and Reyna passed a glance to one another. "Ok, what is going on?" Charlie was clearly becoming frustrated in a very short amount of time.

Seeing the coffee pot, Reyna hopped up, "Anyone need some coffee?"

Right away, Heather said "Yeah."

Hearing nothing from Charlie, Reyna grabbed two coffees, handed one to Heather, and sat back down. Charlie said again, "What is going on?"

"I don't know what you want me to say?" Heather looked at Charlie and then back down at her hands.

"How is Jack doing?" Reyna asked.

Heather looked up with a smile, "He is doing so good."

"Were you able to get him signed up for swimming lessons?" Reyna wanted to keep Heather talking.

"I tried. They said they were full and would put him on a waiting list."

Reyna made notes in her tablet. "Did you let Shirley and Tom know? They were going to check in Winner, I believe, too. Hopefully between the two, we can get him in somewhere."

"No, I haven't talked to them. I don't really want him to do them in Winner, because, right now, I am not sure how I would get there."

"Why wouldn't you be able to get there?" Reyna looked at Charlie. Charlie shrugged her shoulders as if saying 'news to me.'

"My car broke down and I don't have the money to get it fixed."

"You need to tell us these things. We may be able to come up with some resources to help with that." Charlie made another note on her tablet.

Reyna knew there was something Heather wasn't telling them, "How did you get to court today?"

"My Aunt Neen."

"How are you getting home today?"

Heather didn't answer.

"I know it isn't with your Aunt Neen, because I saw her leave the courthouse."

"Bobby said he would be waiting outside for me." Heather leaned over in her chair and laced her hands behind her head.

"What? Bobby is out? When?" Reyna was shocked! She had just talked to him and he was in jail.

"They let him out a couple of days ago for good behavior." Heather didn't look at either of them.

Charlie didn't say a word. She knew she had to choose her words wisely.

"Wow. So, this is why his attorney was confused in court. Even he doesn't know that Bobby is out. So, you're telling me he can come pick you up, but he can't be in court for his own kid?" As Charlie spoke, her words continue to get louder and louder.

Reyna said, "This isn't good."

Heather took a deep breath and said, "He says he can fix my car and will help with Jack."

Right then, Charlie lost it. She emphasized every word as she spoke them. *"What are you talking about? Do you hear yourself right now? Did you hear the judge?"*

Reyna was struggling to know what to say. She remembered the advice her CASA supervisor gave her. *Talk to her with grace.* "Heather, I don't think you should be seen with Bobby. Part of your safety plan *for Jack* is to stay away from Bobby. We thought you were doing so good. Is he clean?"

"He says he is."

"And you believe him?" Charlie is more irritated by the second, "Plus it doesn't matter if you believe him, the judge is under the impression you're split from him. It's one of the conditions of you getting custody of Jack. Why would you jeopardize that? You know I need to put this in my court report. I cannot hide this from the attorneys or the judge." Charlie was frantically making notes. Heather began to cry.

Reyna said, "Call Bobby and tell him you don't need a ride."

"No, I can't do that."

"Can't or won't?"

"Won't!"

"Why not?"

"Because he's on his way."

"So what? Call him and tell him you appreciate him offering but you have a ride home. Explain to him you cannot be seen with him, *especially* in front of the courthouse. Heather, please! What have the last four months been about now to throw it all away?"

Heather looked right at Reyna and said, "Bobby is getting better. Jack needs his dad. I'm doing this for Jack."

"No. You. Are. Not." Charlie truly believed something had to have happened for Heather to be talking like this. Did Bobby get to her? Did he threaten her? This was not the same girl she talked to three days ago. "Get out of my face. I'm so mad right now. I don't want to say something I'll regret. Go."

Reyna refused to give up too easily. Heather stood up to go. "Heather, please think about everything the judge said. This is going to be the hardest fight of your life. Those tough conversations? They start NOW. Please. This doesn't work for us to want this more than you want it for yourself. Do you hear what I'm saying?"

Without saying a word, Heather pushed away from Reyna and ran from the room.

"What the hell was that about?" Charlie pushed her chair away from the table.

"I'm as confused as you. I'm not sure I have witnessed such a blatant disregard for the judge's recommendations as I did just now. I'm in shock."

"I'm pissed!"

Reyna stayed silent, knowing once Charlie processed what just happened, she would come up with a plan.

Charlie looked at Reyna and said, "I didn't think we were going to have to do this, but let's get some brochures together on adoption and set up a meeting with Heather."

Chapter 21

Heather Windsong
November 2019

Heather was trying to stay patient.

It had been three months since Jack had been taken to the Dobson's. At around the two-week mark, Charlie said everything was looking good for Heather. Jack would be returned in no time at all. That was the end of August. And now, three months later, she didn't feel any closer to getting her son back.

She knew Reyna and Charlie were upset with her for getting a ride from Bobby from court. Could they not understand, Bobby was the only one who could fully experience the same feelings she was? They shared the same torment. This was *their* son. This was *their* battle. They were stronger together. She couldn't just turn her back on him when they had been through so much already.

Once Bobby was released from jail, Heather went with him to enroll in AA. And although he never said it to Heather, she was certain this was his rock bottom. He was making his way out. Heather and Jack would be there when he did. Despite the court ordering the two of them to be separated, it didn't take long and Bobby was stopping into McDonald's, bringing her hand written notes. Saying things like, they could get through anything together or asking if she would meet him after her shift.

They would meet at an abandoned house. It sat on the outskirts of town on the opposite end from Aunt Neen, where no one would see them. Bobby would bring a blanket for them to lay on, he brought candles, snacks and cigarettes. Heather would bring the dream catcher and a small pocket bible her Aunt Neen had given her. Bobby would hold her and they would cry together and pray together. He was courting her and Heather yearned for it. They would stay just long enough for him to tenderly love her, each time leaving them both wanting for more.

In those stolen moments, Heather would remind him of how proud of him she was. "I feel our ancestors are guiding us. They are speaking to us, asking us not to make the same mistakes they did."

Bobby would explain how he was feeling. "This time was different being arrested. I had Jack there. I was supposed to protect him... and you. I know if I stay clean, we can make this work. I promise, it's the three of us from here on out." They would wait until just after dark. Bobby would walk her to Aunt Neen's hand in hand, tenderly kissing her before whispering thechilia.[23] Hanhepi.[24]

When she would get home, Heather would cry herself to sleep, waking up several times in the middle of the night because she had dreamed nothing had changed only to wake realizing her whole life had been turned upside down.

Or, the really awful nights, when she would dream that Jack was an adult and didn't remember who she was. Her nights were filled with begging her creator to help them. To save all of them from this nightmare. Her days consisted of going through the motions. Her life of college and pizza making nights with Jack and her friends seemed like a lifetime ago.

***

Aunt Neen struggled with what to say to Heather. Heather's crying was constant. They would be making supper and she would hear whimpering. Heather would be sitting on the floor hugging Hawkeye, crying into his fur. Neen wasn't sure when it went from

---

23 I love you

24 Good night

her and Heather fighting to get Jack back to Heather and Bobby. Neen tried to reconcile her feelings between the Bobby she had known to the person he said he was now.

Neen wanted to believe for her niece's sake that he had changed. However, Neen had accidentally walked up on him when he was in a heated conversation on his phone. He was constantly texting. When questioned, it was always his boss. Bobby joked about how he was practically running the construction company by himself. According to Bobby, he had no friends other than her and Heather, so, it must have been his work, right? Heather pleaded with her aunt to give him one more chance. Neen was definitely trying. Heather reiterated to her aunt all of the things he was doing to fight for them. Couldn't Auntie see? Their prayers were being answered. If her aunt and others didn't see that, then Heather would help them.

Heather had tried calling her attorney multiple times and hadn't received a call back. More than anything, Heather wanted Jack home before the holiday season started. Elder Miller hosted Heather, Aunt Neen, and Lola for Thanksgiving. He spoiled them with a wonderful meal. Heather appreciated them all coming together for her. And although she tried to stay positive, she couldn't help her thoughts going to Bobby and if he was spending the day alone. Celebrating Thanksgiving without him and Jack was hard enough. They had originally thought they would have Jack for the day, but there wasn't enough DSS workers available to help transport him and the Dobsons were out of town. Heather wondered if it wasn't all done on purpose to prove a point.

When the judge spoke to her in court about making hard choices, she was listening. And she was doing everything they told her she needed to do to get custody of Jack. She was going to the jail every morning and night for her breathalyzer. She hadn't missed a shift at work. She was early for the visits with Jack and never missed a parent meeting with her counselor. She was doing every single thing she was asked. The only thing she wasn't doing was staying away from Bobby. She was certain Charlie had told the judge. Could the courts punish her by keeping Jack from her?

Heather remained adamant, if she could keep Bobby clean and get Jack back from foster care, then they would move back to Mitchell and, this time, they would stay there. And although Heather hadn't said anything for a few months, she was still looking for a place in Mitchell that would be big enough for Aunt Neen to live with them as well. Heather was working hard for their future. She was determined to stay on the straight and narrow this time. Heather's goal was to coincide Jack's return with Aunt Neen feeling better and them being back in Mitchell by the start of summer semester.

Aunt Neen had recently struggled with some respiratory issues. When Elder Miller called Heather and asked about hosting, she knew it was just as much for Aunt Neen as it was for her. Elder Miller kept proving over and over again, what a strong, Lakota man looked like. Again, she wished Bobby could be here to witness it, to learn from it.

Heather kept feeling as if time was of the essence. Every day Jack wasn't with them was a day lost of laughter, snuggles, and memories. Heather blamed herself for her aunt not feeling well. And she felt a broken heart was attributing to her aunt's illness, even though the doctor assured them it was respiratory and treatable. With everything going on, Heather continued to do the only thing she could. She kept walking towards her future, her thokata.[25]

---

25 Future

Part Three

"What if Your blessings come

through raindrops?

What if Your healing comes through tears?

What if a thousand sleepless nights are what

it takes to know Your near?

And what if trials of this life are Your mercies

in disguise?"

~ Blessings, Laura Story

Chapter 22

Heather counted down the minutes to get to their meeting spot. She couldn't wait to feel his arms around her.

The first time he didn't show, she sat in that abandoned, smelly, dark run-down shack for hours waiting for him. The second time, he asked if she could meet right after work. After 10 minutes of getting there, he had texted her, saying he couldn't make it and his phone was about to die. But he was sorry and would try to make it up to her.

Heather knew something was going on. She saw the signs, but she ignored them. She also denied anything was going on to anyone that questioned her about it. She didn't want Aunt Neen, Lola, or Elder Miller looking at her with pity.

Bobby wouldn't answer her calls or wouldn't call her back for days at a time. When he would call her, he sounded high and was always defensive. Charlie called her and asked if Bobby had gotten a new number, because she was unable to get a hold of him. Heather told Charlie he had been working a lot and probably got busy. His employer called her one morning asking if she could get a message to him because he had missed work several days in a row. Heather said he had been sick. She was willing to make excuses for him and lie for him, except when it came to him missing his visits with Jack. That was where she drew the line.

Originally, when Charlie and Reyna questioned if these visits were in the best interest of Jack, she said, yes. As long as the visits were monitored, Heather felt strongly that Bobby needed those visits to encourage his sobriety. When Bobby missed a visit and when the visitation center called her or if Charlie or Reyna called her, Heather would say he was at work or she just wouldn't answer the phone. Heather had been down this road countless times before, however, this time was different. This time she had a plan. And this plan did not include breaking down or mourning a future that had not been theirs to begin with.

She had just parked her car to go into work when she saw she was getting a call from an inmate at the county jail. She had been expecting this call. She thought it would be full of excuses and empty apologies. She wasn't prepared for the sobs and broken words he was saying. He ended the call with asking her if she would come see him. By the time Bobby had called Heather, she already knew what had happened.

Reyna had called Heather earlier that day, "I wanted you to hear this from me, before the gossips got to you."

"I knew something was wrong. How bad is it? What's he done this time?"

"It's bad. He was picked up in Mitchell. He-- Heather, I don't know how to say this. He almost beat a girl to death."

"What?!?"

"It gets worse. He had cocaine on him. And when they got a warrant for his car, there was more in there. A lot more. They're—they're charging him with possession with intent to distribute, in addition to attempted murder."

Bobby had been picked up in Mitchell. As soon as Heather hung up the phone from Reyna, another friend was calling asking her if she had heard, shortly after that there was an article in the online paper, and that evening his picture was on each of the local news stations. Everything was a blur. And, once again, her world had been turned upside down.

Bobby asked her to come see him in Mitchell at the public safety building, where they were holding him until his court appearance. She agreed. So, here she was. They were allowed to sit at the same table, the table was metal and round. It felt like a cafeteria; the only difference was that there were bars on the partitions that surrounded them. It was a bright area, almost too bright. One bulb was flickering above them. Heather saw a program on TV where they actually had the bulb flicker on purpose. It kept the inmates on edge.

Bobby was already sitting at the table when Heather walked in. He had on a dark blue jump suit; he was sitting hunched over with his hands folded in his lap. His ankles and wrists were shackled. Heather winced at the sight of them, remembering back to when she wore her own set.

Without lifting his head, he said, "Thechihila ksto."[26]

Heather could feel the shield of Aunt Neen around her, keeping her resolve strong, she said to him, "You promised! You promised me this time would be different! You can't even look at me." Bobby didn't move. "Fuck you! Fuck. You." Her voice lowered to a whisper, "I hate you." Heather's hands were shaking.

Rather than allowing herself to feel sadness or fear for the future, she felt anger. Her words were jumbled in her head. She had wondered if coming to see Bobby before they transported him would be a good idea but she knew she needed closure. Aunt Neen had given her blessing and reminded Heather to think of nothing else but Jack.

"I'm not sure why you asked me here. And, honestly, I'm not sure why I came. I guess I want you to know, I can't do this anymore. For Jack's sake, I need to be done. The days of kastoya[27] are

---

26 I love you

27 Loving you

over. From this point forward I now choose me, our son, and the beautiful life I am going to create."

Heather didn't mean for it to happen, but she found herself talking Lakota to him. She could feel her ancestors talking through her trying to reach him. "Don't you see? You are leaving me to do this all on my own? Why? You had me and you had the best little boy! What happens if I don't get Jack? And then I am alone? And yet, I don't want to give up. Why did you? Are the drugs that important? I begged the spirits of the past to let you go! I pleaded with the Spirit World to make you a strong, Lakota man for your family- for me – for your son – for you! My heart is breaking and I am lost. And I do not want to feel this way anymore. And I do not want our son to ever feel this way. I am done feeling darkness. I now want to be the light. The light for our son and our future. This is goodbye."

To her surprise he reached for her hand. He sat there for a long time with his head down but still holding her hand. He looked up, his eyes a brilliant green. His words came out slowly. "Did you know your Auntie called me and asked me to be at Thanksgiving? I couldn't do it. I couldn't bring myself to go there and spend the day with you and *our* family." Bobby took a deep breath. "That is when I knew I couldn't be the man you needed." Again, he paused, "After I was arrested this last time, Elder Miller came to see me. He asked if I could give you just one gift before I say goodbye to you forever. He asked me to tell you why I can't be the man you need." He spoke to her in their Native language. "I am broken and I don't know why. I must be the one to let you go. Perhaps we will meet again someday in the wanagi-macoce.[28] For that will be the only place our love will bloom again as it did back in the story-telling days. Until now, my love for you has not been evident in my actions. Today, it will be. Today, I choose you and I choose Jack. This is *my* way of loving you. Goodbye my Wowastelake,[29] my whole world."

---

28 Spirit world

29 Love

Before Heather had a chance to respond, Bobby was standing up and walked to the guard. Heather wanted to scream, "No! One more touch! Just one more. Please, don't leave me, don't leave us!" But she remained silent and let the tears flow. She welcomed these tears. The tears she thought had left her. The tears that washed away the sorrow and the brokenness and instead brought new dreams, new purpose.

CHAPTER 23

It was the middle of December, two weeks after the last court hearing, when Heather received a call from Charlie asking if her and Reyna would be able to stop by. They wanted to go over the court packet with her. When Heather received the call, Jack had just left with Shirley Dobson. Her emotions were twisted inside her. Once again, following the visit, she was a bawling mess. Heather remembered back to getting that first phone call from Charlie and the first phone call from Reyna. She had been so depressed, they probably thought there was no hope for her. Now, at least she knew the both of them. And she truly did get the impression they were both in it to help her. Before Charlie hung up the phone, she asked if it would be possible to have Aunt Neen there as well. Heather quickly called Aunt Neen to let her know what was going on.

"Auntie - Charlie just called. Her and Reyna want to meet with us at two today at home. Please tell me you can be there?"

"Of course, I will be there. I will run to the store and grab some tea and shortbread cookies. Can you think of anything else we will need?"

"Maybe some diet coke? I think they both like drinking that."

This gave Heather time to get back to Neen's and have some time to gather her thoughts. *I wonder why both of them are coming? To go over the court packet? The next court date isn't until January. Why are they coming now? Something is wrong.* Heather took the time to look presentable. She touched up her makeup and tidied up the house. She wasn't letting her guard down. She thought of the conversation she had with Aunt Neen so many months ago. *You must prove to them you are the best mommy.*

Aunt Neen had run to the grocery store to pick up the supplies they had talked about, she was also feeling the need make a good impression. Charlie and Reyna arrived at exactly 2 pm.

They all made their way to the kitchen and sat down, each taking a side of the table. After a little chit-chat and a pause in the conversation, Charlie said, "You're probably wondering why we called to ask you to meet with us."

"Yes. Is everything ok?" If Heather was worried before, she was really worried now. She saw a look pass between Charlie and Reyna and she caught a glimpse of a brochure Charlie was holding. It read: Adoption – Making Children's Future Bright.

Very rarely is an emergency court called for a good reason. Heather stood at the elevator doors on the first floor. Her heart was beating out of her chest. This was the normal feeling she got when she stood at these silver doors. To get to the second floor for family court, she had to walk through the hallway that connected the public entrance to the prison entrance. Once she turned the corner, she was at the elevator doors. If she were to go straight, past the breathalyzer counter, she would find her home away from home for those three days back in July. She had been here for her review hearings, but today it was different. Perhaps it was different because just a few short days ago, Bobby was housed here. This jail/courthouse was where she said good bye to her old life and to the love of her life. She prayed the judge sees it the same way. Heather reminded herself to remain calm and to think only of Jack. As if reading her mind, Aunt Neen whispered in her ear, "Peace, niecie."

Charlie had reiterated to Heather multiple times that this emergency hearing could very well be a good thing. As Heather and

Aunt Neen entered the court room, Heather took her spot next to her attorney and Aunt Neen sat directly behind her. Heather could feel the solidarity surrounding her.

Today Heather wore her hair up in a high bun. She had worn light makeup. She wore a sherpa sweater because it was Jack's favorite. It was ultra-soft, and he loved to snuggle with her when she wore it. She wore her favorite dark blue jeans.

Charlie and Reyna came in together. Heather glanced up and gave them a small smile. Although they couldn't guarantee what this hearing was about, and Charlie didn't say exactly, Heather remained hopeful but apprehensive. She didn't want to assume too much too soon.

Originally when this all began back in July, they thought she would have Jack back in a few weeks, and here, six months later, it could finally be happening. Heather looked around. The State's Attorney sat at the opposite table. Next to her sat Jack's attorney. The court reporter was sitting directly in front of the judge's chair. Charlie was up front and center, perched on the edge of her seat, prepared for battle if needed. The ICWA representative was not present. Reyna sat next to Neen.

Neen grabbed Reyna's hand and gave it a quick squeeze. The buzz in the courtroom went to a dead silence when Judge Jones opened the chamber door. "All rise!" The bailiff's voice echoed throughout the courtroom.

As the judge entered, Heather could feel herself start to shake. She looked behind her first at Charlie and then back to Aunt Neen and Reyna. All three of them gave her a weak smile. The judge went through the standard protocol and then directed his attention to Heather. "In our family court system, we see many different scenarios come through and many different outcomes. As a judge I am presented often times with some really tough decisions. This case was no different."

The crisp, South Dakota air met them in celebration. Heather, Neen, Charlie, and Reyna gathered outside the courthouse, taking turns hugging Heather. "Now that you will be moving back to Mitchell, we can see you a little more."

Heather laughed, "Not to sound ungrateful, but I don't necessarily want to see *more* of you guys! But seriously, I do want to thank you both for everything you have done."

Heather turned towards Charlie, "Are we OK to go meet the Dobsons and pick up Ja-Jack?" Heather looked at her Aunt Neen as she said it. Her voice cracked when she said Jack's name.

Charlie was pulling her stocking cap on her head. "Yes, they texted me and said they are at McDonald's. They are expecting you. Remember, this is a very emotional day for them as well."

"Ok. That sounds good. I can't wait to thank them for the incredible letter they wrote to the judge on my behalf. And Auntie, the letter you wrote, thank you so, so much."

Aunt Neen looked to Reyna and then to Charlie, "It was because of these two. I had asked what I could do to help and they said to write about the Heather I know. That was easy enough. And I knew Elder Miller and Lola would want to help, so they wrote one too. That reminds me, I do need to text him." Aunt Neen gave a quick hug to both Reyna and Charlie. She turned to Heather. "I'll meet you in the car." Charlie turned to follow Aunt Neen, "I'll walk with you. Heather, I'll see you soon."

Reyna gave Heather a quick hug, "Well, I guess it's time to say goodbye. I'm so proud of you. Please keep in touch and let me know if there is anything you need." Reyna started to walk to her car. She turned around and said, "Heather?"

"Yes?"

"Can you do me a favor? Give Jack a big hug for me?" Reyna smiled.

Heather smiled in return, "I can definitely do that."

As Reyna walked to her car, she sent up a quick prayer asking for the Holy Spirit to be with every single one of them today and for all the days to come.

Heather sat in the driver's seat, started the car, and folded her hands. She took a deep breath. She was feeling so many emotions. She had just received the best news, so, what was this overwhelming need to cry? She was thinking of everything that had happened up until this point. She was trying to imagine how Jack would feel knowing he now got to live with her again.

Aunt Neen reached for Heather's hand. "Niecie, let me tell you something before we go. We share many of the same ancestors, you and I. Our past no longer defines us. We are a beautiful, strong people. These last couple of months you have proven that to everyone. I am so proud to be your Auntie. I love you and will always be your greatest ally. Now, we take it day by day. We are going to plan for one heck of a Christmas with our boy."

Aunt Neen gave a little giggle and sat back in the passenger seat. Heather also smiled, started the car, and drove to her future. Tracy Chapman's "Fast Car" was playing on the radio. She turned it up and started singing along.

Although, their intent was to spend most of their time in Mitchell for the holidays, they decided to go home first. They both wanted Jack's memories of the reservation as safe and joyful ones. Christmas that year was like no other. The three of them spent three days decorating and baking. They decorated inside and out. Aunt Neen decorated the yard with a blow-up Santa Claus and reindeer that took up most of the yard. They really were creating a Hallmark movie.

More than once, Heather found herself dropping to her knees and thanking Jesus for this second chance. As if just for them, they had a beautiful snowfall every few days and mild weather for the

Dakotas. For New Year's, Aunt Neen surprised Heather and Jack with tickets to Disney on Ice's "New Year Magic" performance, in which they were able to spend the weekend in Omaha. Lola met them there and brought good news with her. The 'Walk America Clean' campaign had received a huge grant. They would be back in Omaha in a couple of months strategizing and collaborating with the Nebraska and South Dakota Governors.

Heather couldn't remember a time when she was happier than she was now, and the thought of Aunt Neen going with them to Mitchell gave her a sense of peace and calm for the future.

They made sure to send pictures periodically to the Dobsons. The love they showed and the bond that was forged while Jack lived with them would always be there. Heather could either be a part of that bond or not.

She decided for Jack's sake, to love them, because they loved him.

Thank You

The fact that I am even writing this has me feeling like anything is possible! Writing this book was one of the hardest and most rewarding things I have ever done in my life.

I want to thank first and foremost my daughter, Taylor Mohr for always reading what I wrote and giving me feedback from the very beginning, all the way to the very end. I love you, respect you, and adore you.

I want to thank Teresa Hart, Kelly Knippling, Sue Hanson, Lila Eilts, Cindy Doctor, Shawna Veenker, Kelly O'Malley, Kate Hart, Kelsi Hart, and Jessica Werner for being some of the first people that knew I was writing this and filled me up with so much encouragement.

I want to thank my mom for sending me articles and books that she knew would inspire me. Thank you for the early morning talks and being my biggest cheerleader throughout my whole life, and especially with this project.

I want to thank my dad for loving Dances with Wolves as much as I do. Thank you for showing me how selfless love can be. You and mom gave us kids the most magical life in beautiful South Dakota. Thank you. I love you both so much.

I want to thank my Aunt Eileen for encouraging me to continue with this project even when I had doubts. Aunt Eileen – Thank you for asking me to participate in that writing prompt so many years ago. Thank you for sharing your wisdom, incredible talent, and time with me. Our love for writing has created an extraordinary bond and I am so grateful.

Dwayne Senstrom and Peg Diekhoff – Thank you for giving me a new way to look at the Native American culture and for being so patient with my questions. Thank you, Dwayne, for reminding me why words matter. CASA will forever be coined as Impartial Advisor for me. You gave me so much to think about.

Thank you to Ally Fallon, Lauren Kinney, Candance Hurkman, Julie Walton, and Shelby Olufson for being the best writing circle and professionals a girl could ask for!

Thank you, Laura Duffy for the amazing work you did with my pitch and original book cover. You are unbelievably talented, and I look forward to working with you again.

Thank you, Mark Cornelius for the advice and "writer's talk." I am one of your biggest fans! A special shout out to Dan Anderson for introducing us.

Thank you to Michael Lee with NCACIA for understanding why this book was so important for me to write and fine tuning my police report. What you are doing for our children is so important and I am super grateful to have met you.

Thank you to my children and grandchildren for being my motivation for everything I do.

Thank you to Doug for allowing me so many hours of just writing. Thank you for always being willing to sit right beside me and just be there, even though I would say, "No talking, I am writing."

Thank you to my email group and the many, many kind words of encouragement I receive on a weekly basis. It was with your encouragement that I made it across the finish line!

And a big thank you to Ellen Rogin for introducing me to the best in the business! Ben, Lexi, and Mish with Hambone Publishing – you are rockstars!!! Thank you for taking a chance with me and thank you for working tirelessly to meet the deadlines. I appreciate your professionalism and friendship so much!

And lastly, thank you to Bonnie Scott, Jackie Horton, and Macey Bohl for your guidance on all of my CASA cases. And thank you to the CASA volunteers, DSS workers, police officers, and judges for working together for our youth.

Thank you, my good and faithful God, for always, incessantly nudging me, reminding me that writing, for me, is like breathing.

And to all of my CASA kids. You are my heroes.

WHAT YOU CAN DO

Thank you so much for reading *Because They Loved Him*. This book was written by me with all my imperfections–but also with all my love. I'm deeply grateful to the organizations listed below, whose guidance helped make this story possible.

If you feel inspired to learn more or get involved, I encourage you to explore the websites linked below.

If you enjoyed *Because They Loved Him*, I'd be so grateful if you left a review on Amazon, Google, Goodreads or shared your thoughts on social media. Be sure to tag me—my LinkTree is listed below. I read and truly appreciate every review and post.

Thank you!
Traci Kay Davis

South Dakota CASA:

NCACIA:

Native Hope/MMIW:

Traci's LinkTree: